Desert Prince Docs

Doctors, brothers…sheikhs!

When not exercising their expert talents in
A&E, Princes Zahir and Dakan Al Rahal are
renowned throughout their kingdom for their
honour, integrity and dazzling good looks!
Their focus is on their work—until they
encounter two unexpected distractions…

Now, sweet, funny nurse Adele Jenson
and feisty temptress Nira Hathaway
are about to prove to these royal docs
that commanding a kingdom is
easier than conquering their desires!

Find out what happens in:

Zahir & Adele's story
Seduced by the Sheikh Surgeon
by Carol Marinelli

and

Dakan & Nira's story
Challenging the Doctor Sheikh
by Amalie Berlin

Available now!

Dear Reader,

I love writing sheikh romances, so I was thrilled to be asked to write the first in a duo with the lovely Amalie Berlin.

My hero, Zahir Al Rahal, is the eldest of two brothers. Both are royal and both are doctors, yet they have very different personalities. Zahir is rather more formal and austere than his younger brother, Dakan, and I rather like that about him. So too does my heroine, Adele.

Of course Zahir is completely unattainable, and he really doesn't even seem to notice Adele, yet he is the go-to place in her head—a lovely daydream that has helped her through some very difficult times. No matter how she fights it and tries to move on, he remains her secret crush. Or perhaps it's not such a secret after all!

Happy reading,

Carol x

SEDUCED
BY THE
SHEIKH SURGEON

BY
CAROL MARINELLI

First published in Great Britain 2016
By Mills & Boon, an imprint of HarperCollins*Publishers*
1 London Bridge Street, London, SE1 9GF

Large Print edition 2017

© 2016 Carol Marinelli

ISBN: 978-0-263-06677-7

Carol Marinelli recently filled in a form asking for her job title. Thrilled to be able to put down her answer, she put 'writer'. Then it asked what Carol did for relaxation and she put down the truth—'writing'. The third question asked for her hobbies. Well, not wanting to look obsessed, she crossed her fingers and answered 'swimming'—but, given that the chlorine in the pool does terrible things to her highlights, I'm sure you can guess the real answer!

Books by Carol Marinelli

Mills & Boon Medical Romance

The Hollywood Hills Clinic
Seduced by the Heart Surgeon

Midwives On-Call
Just One Night?

Baby Twins to Bind Them
The Baby of Their Dreams
The Socialite's Secret

Mills & Boon Modern Romance

Irresistible Russian Tycoons
The Price of His Redemption
The Cost of the Forbidden
Billionaire Without a Past
Return of the Untamed Billionaire

Visit the Author Profile page at millsandboon.co.uk for more titles.

CHAPTER ONE

IT WASN'T BECAUSE of lack of opportunity for there had been plenty of them.

In fact, here was one now!

A late spring storm had come from nowhere and lit up the London sky.

Adele stood at the bus stop across the road from the Accident and Emergency department, where she had just finished working a late shift. The rain battered the shelter and she would probably be better off standing behind it. Her white dress, which was not designed to get wet, clung to her and had shrunk to mid-thigh and her shoulder-length blond hair was plastered to her head.

She wore no mascara so she was safe there—Adele wouldn't be greeting Zahir with panda eyes.

It was ten at night and she could see the blinkers on his silver sports car as he drove out of the hospital, turned right and drove towards her.

Surely now? Adele thought, as she stepped out from the supposed shelter just to make sure that she could be seen.

Surely any decent human being who saw a colleague standing shivering and wet at a bus stop, caught in a sudden storm, would slow down and offer them a lift home.

And when he did Adele would smile and say, 'Thank you,' and get into the car. Zahir would see her clinging dress and wonder how the hell he had not noticed the junior nurse in *that* way before.

And she would forgive him for a year of rudely ignoring her. Finally alone, they would make conversation and as they pulled up at her flat...

Adele hadn't quite worked out that part. She loathed her flat and flatmates and couldn't really see Zahir in there.

Maybe he would suggest a drink back at his place, Adele thought as finally, *finally*, her moment came and the silver car slowed down.

She actually started to walk towards it, so certain was she that their moment had come.

But then he picked up speed and drove on.

No, his car didn't splash her with water, but she felt the drenching of his repeated rejection, just as if it had.

He must have just slowed down to turn on his radio or something, Adele soon realised, for Zahir drove straight past her.

How could she fancy someone as unfeeling as him? she wondered.

It was a conundrum she regularly wrangled with.

She couldn't console herself that he didn't like women.

Zahir dated.

A lot.

On too many occasions Adele had sat at the nurses' station or in the staffroom as he'd taken a call from whoever his latest perturbed girlfriend had been.

Perturbed because it was Saturday night and they were supposed to be out and Zahir was at work. Perturbed because it was Sunday afternoon and he had said several hours ago that he was only popping in to work.

Work was his priority. That much was clear.

During Adele's last set of night shifts he had been called in when he hadn't been rostered on. Wherever he had come from had required him to wear a tux. He had looked divine. For once he had been utterly clean shaven and his thick black hair had been slicked back. Adele had tried to stammer out the problem with the patient that she and Janet, the nurse unit manager, had been concerned about.

It had proved to be a hard ask.

'He was seen here this afternoon and discharged with antibiotics,' Adele said. 'His mother's still concerned and has brought him back tonight. The paediatrician has seen him again and explained it's too soon for the antibiotics to take effect.'

'What is your concern?' Zahir asked.

His cologne was heavy yet it could not douse the testosterone and sexual energy that was almost a visible aura to Adele. His deep, gravelly voice asked pertinent questions about the patient. She loved his rich accent and each stroke of a vowel he delivered went straight to her thighs.

'Adele,' he asked again, 'what is the main reason for your concern?'

'The mother's very worried,' Adele said, and closed her eyes because mothers were always very worried. 'And so am I.'

Zahir had gone in to examine the patient when a stunning woman had walked into the department. Her long brown hair and make-up were perfect despite the late hour. Dressed in silver, she had marched up to Janet and asked in a very bossy voice exactly how long Zahir would be.

'Bella, I said to wait in the car.' Zahir's curt response had made the beauty jump. Clearly she only spoke like this out of his earshot.

Janet smothered a smile as Bella stalked off. 'Gone by morning,' she said to Adele.

Zahir had asked that Janet send in Helene to assist him.

More experience was required.

Adele had none.

Well, not with men but it seriously irked her that even after a year of working in Accident and Emergency he seemed to treat her as if she had just started.

And she had been right to be worried about the child.

Zahir performed a lumbar puncture and viral meningitis was later confirmed. The little boy was admitted and ended up staying in hospital for five days.

Not that Zahir told her.

There was never any follow-up for Adele.

And yet, for all his faults in the communication department, Zahir was the highlight of her working day.

Of all her days.

Well, no more, she decided as his car glided past.

He was arrogant and dismissive and it had been outright mean of him not to stop and offer her a lift—she refused to fancy him any longer.

Adele's world was small, too small, she knew that and was determined to do something about it.

The bus finally arrived.

Actually, two of them did. The one that was late and the one that was due.

Spoiled for choice, Adele thought as she climbed onto the emptier one and said hello to the driver.

There were some of the regulars on board and there were a few others.

Adele was a regular and knew she could zone out for the next half-hour. She rested her head against the window as the bus hissed and jolted its way through the rain, and as it did so she went to her favourite place in the world.

Zahir.

Her conundrum.

She had no choice in her attraction toward him, she had long since decided. She had fought it, tried to deny it, tried to do something about it and she had also tried to ignore it.

Yet it persisted.

It simply existed and she had to somehow learn to live alongside it.

Maybe it was because he was completely unobtainable, she considered as someone started to sing at the back of the bus.

Yes, she needed to get out more and she was starting to do so. On Friday night she had a first date with Paul—a paramedic who had made his interest in her clear.

Just say yes, everyone at work had told her.

Finally she had.

Except it wasn't Paul that she wanted to go out with.

It was, and felt as if it always would be, Zahir.

His name badge read, 'Zahir, Emergency Consultant.'

The patients did not need to know he was Crown Prince Sheikh Zahir Al Rahal, of Mamlakat Almas.

Her heart hadn't needed to know that either. She had felt its rate quicken the moment she had seen him, before she had even known his name.

At first sight, even before their first introduction, this odd feeling had taken residence in Adele.

His hair was black and glossy, and his skin was the colour of caramel and just as enticing. The paper gown he'd worn had strained over wide shoulders. There had been an air of control in the resuscitation room even though it had been clear that the patient's situation had been dire.

He had glanced up from the patient he'd been treating and for a second his silver-grey eyes had met Adele's and she had felt her cheeks grow warm under his brief gaze.

'I'm just showing Adele around the department.' Janet, the nurse unit manager conducting the interview, had explained.

He had given just the briefest of nods and then he had got back to treating the critical patient.

'As you can see, the resuscitation area has been updated since you were last here,' Janet had said. 'We've now got five beds and two cots.'

Yes, it had been updated but the basics had been the same.

Adele had stood for a moment, remembering a time, several years previously, when she had been wheeled in here and, given that Janet had been with her on that awful day, she had perhaps understood why Adele had been quiet.

Janet had made no reference to it, though; in fact, as they'd both walked back towards Janet's office she'd spoken of other things.

'That was Zahir, one of our emergency consultants,' Janet said. 'You'll have come across him when you did your placement.'

'No.' Adele shook her head. 'He wasn't here then. I believe he was on leave.'

'He's been working here for a couple of years now but, yes, he is away quite a lot. Zahir has a lot of commitments back home so he works on temporary contracts,' Janet explained. 'We always cross our fingers that he'll renew. He's a huge asset to the department.

'I've worked with his brother, Dakan,' Adele said.

They both shared a smile.

Dakan had just completed his residency and was a bit wild and cheeky, and she knew from the hospital grapevine that Zahir was the more austere of the two.

Of course she had heard about his brooding dark looks and yet she had never expected him to be quite so attractive.

Adele hadn't really found anyone that attractive before.

Not that it mattered.

There had been no room in her life for that sort of thing, not that Zahir would even give her a second glance.

'So,' Janet said as they headed back to her office, 'are you still keen to work here?'

'Very.' Adele nodded. 'I never thought I'd want to work in Emergency but during my placement I found that I loved it…'

'And you're very good at it. You shall have to work in Resus, though.'

'I understand that.'

As a student nurse Adele had struggled through her Accident and Emergency placement. She had dreaded going into the room where, even though her mother hadn't died, Adele had found out that she was lost to her.

Janet, knowing all that had gone on, had been

very patient and had given Adele the minimum time in Resus and had looked out for her when she was there. Now, though, if Adele wanted to make Accident and Emergency her specialty, there could be no kid-glove treatment.

'Are you sure it won't be too much for you?' Janet checked.

'I'm sure.' Adele nodded. She had given it a lot of thought and she explained what she had come to realise during her training.

'Really, my mother was in Theatre, in Radiology and ICU. For some reason the Resus room hit me the hardest but I've come to understand that there are memories of that time all over the place.'

'How is Lorna doing now?' Janet asked carefully.

'She's still the same.' Adele gave a strained smile. 'She's in a really lovely nursing home, the staff are just wonderful and I go in and see her at least once a day.'

'That's a lot of pressure.'

'Not really.' Adele shook her head. 'I'm not sure

if she knows I'm there but I'd hate her to think I'd forgotten her.'

Janet wanted to say something.

Years of visiting her mother at *least* once a day would take its toll, she knew.

But then Janet understood why it would be so hard for Adele to move on. After all, she knew the details of the accident.

Janet had been working that day.

They had been alerted that there had been a motor-vehicle accident and that there had been five people injured and in the process of being freed from the wreckage of the cars.

Lorna Jenson, a front-seat passenger, had been in critical condition with severe head and chest injuries.

The driver of the other car had abdominal and head injuries and had been brought into Resus too. His wife and daughter had escaped with minor injuries but they had been hysterical and their screams and tears had filled the department.

And finally, as Lorna had been about to be taken to Theatre for surgery to hopefully relieve the pressure on her brain, Janet had gone in to speak with her eighteen-year-old daughter who'd lain staring at the ceiling.

Adele's blonde hair had been splattered with blood and her face had been as white as the pillow. Her china-blue eyes had not blinked, they'd just stared up at the ceiling and her lips too had been white.

'Adele?' Janet checked, and Adele attempted to give a small nod but she was wearing a hard cervical collar. 'Can you tell me your full name?' Janet asked as she checked the wristband. She had been busy dealing with the critically injured patient and had to be very sure to whom she was speaking.

'Adele Jenson.'

'Good.' Having confirmed to whom she was speaking, Janet pressed on. 'I believe that Phillip, the consultant, has been in and spoken with you about your mother.'

'He has,' Adele said.

Phillip had been in and had gently told her just how unwell her mother was and that there was a real possibility that she might not make it through the operation.

His glasses had fogged up as he'd looked down at Adele and told her the grim news.

Adele didn't understand how the doctor had tears in his eyes and yet hers were dry.

Now Janet was looking down at her.

'She's going to be going to Theatre very soon.'

'How's the man…?' Adele asked.

'I'm sorry, Adele, I can't give you that information.'

'I can hear his family crying.'

'I know you can.'

'How badly are they hurt?'

'I'm sorry, Adele. Again, I can't give you that information, it's to do with patient confidentiality.'

'I know it is,' Adele said. 'I'm a nursing student. But I just need to know how he is, if he's alive.'

'It's very hard for you.' Janet gave her hand a little squeeze but gave her no information. 'I wondered if you'd like me to take you in to see your mother before she goes up to Theatre.'

Adele tried to sit up.

'Just lie there,' Janet soothed. 'We'll wheel you over on the gurney. I can take that collar off you now, Phillip just checked your X-rays and says your neck is fine. It just had to be put on as a precaution.'

Gently she removed it.

'How do you feel?' Janet asked.

'I'm fine,' Adele said, though, in fact, she felt sick and had the most terrible headache, possibly from sitting in the car as the firefighters had used the Jaws of Life to peel back the roof. The noise had been deafening. The silence from her mother beside her had been far worse, though.

Janet could hear the sound of police radios outside the curtain and one of them asking if they could speak with Adele Jenson.

'Just one moment,' Janet said to Adele. She took the police to the far end of the corridor, well out of Adele's earshot.

'I'm just about to take her in to see her mother. Can this wait for a little while?'

'Of course,' the officer agreed. 'But we really do need to speak with the other driver.'

'*Learner* driver,' Janet said, and with that one word she asked that they tread very carefully.

The officer nodded.

Janet left them then and wheeled Adele in to see her mother.

At the time Janet was quite sure Lorna wouldn't make it through surgery.

But she did.

Now Lorna clung to life in a chronic vegetative state.

And her daughter, Janet rightly guessed, was still paying the price for that terrible day.

CHAPTER TWO

'THAT WAS SOME storm last night,' Janet said.

'You're telling me!' Helene responded. 'Hayden was driving and I had to get him to pull over.'

Adele was on another late shift and they were sitting at the nurses' station. They had been discussing annual leave before the conversation had been sidetracked.

Adele really wasn't in the mood to hear about Helene's son's driving lessons.

Again!

Helene had, a few months ago, come back to nursing after a long break away to raise her perfect family, and she spoke about them all the time.

'Did you get home okay, Adele?' Janet checked.

'I did,' Adele said, glancing over at Zahir, who had his back to her and was checking lab results on the computer. He was wearing navy scrubs and his long legs were stretched out. He was still taking up far too much space in her mind. 'A lovely man stopped and gave me a lift.'

She watched as Zahir briefly stopped scrolling through results but then he resumed.

'Who, Paul?' Janet asked, because they all knew that Adele had a date with him tomorrow night.

'No.' Adele shook her head. 'It was just some random man. As it turned out, he'd escaped from police guard in the psychiatric unit, but I didn't feel threatened—he didn't have his chainsaw with him.'

Janet laughed. She understood Adele's slightly off-the-wall humour. 'You got the bus, then.'

'Yes, I got the bus.'

Chatter break over, they got back to business.

'Adele, you really need to take some annual leave.'

Janet placed the annual leave roster in front of her and Adele frowned as Janet explained. 'Admin don't like us to hold too much over and further you haven't taken any in the time you've been here.'

'Nice problem to have!' Helene said.

'What about September?' Adele suggested, because there were several slots there and Janet nodded and pencilled a fortnight in then. 'You need to take two weeks before that, though.'

The trouble with that was it was now May. The upcoming summer months were all taken. In fact, a couple of months ago Adele had cancelled her leave when Helene had won a competition to take her perfect family on an overseas holiday.

'How about the first two weeks of June?' Janet suggested. 'There's a spot there.'

'But that's only three weeks away.'

'That will give you time to book something last minute and cheap,' Janet said. 'I've been telling you to take some leave for ages, Adele.'

She had been.

'What might you do?' Helene asked once Janet had gone.

'I have no idea,' Adele admitted.

The truth was, even if she could afford to jet

off to somewhere nice, she could not bear the thought of leaving behind her mum.

And a fortnight without the routine of work wasn't something that Adele wanted either.

She didn't like the flat where she lived, and, feeling guilty about acknowledging it to herself, neither did she want to spend even more time at the nursing home.

Perhaps she could do some agency work and try to get enough money together to start looking for her own place.

'How is Mr Richards now, Adele?' Zahir asked about the patient whose notes she had been catching up on when the subject of annual leave had arisen.

'He's comfortable.'

'And how are his obs?'

'Stable,' Adele said.

Mr Richards was on half-hourly obs and they were due, oh, one and half minutes from now.

Basically, Zahir was prompting her to do them.

Well, she didn't need him to remind her, as he

so often did, but she said nothing and hopped down from her stool.

Mr Richards had unstable angina and as she did the observations Adele smiled down at the old man, who was all curled up under his blanket and grumbling as the blood-pressure cuff inflated.

'I want to sleep.'

'I know that you do,' Adele said, 'but we need to keep a close eye on you for now.'

His blood pressure had gone up and his heart rate was elevated. 'Do you have any pain at the moment?' Adele asked.

'None, or I wouldn't have, if you'd just let me sleep.'

Adele went to tell Zahir about the changes but was halted by a very elegant woman. She had a ripple of long black hair that trailed down her back and she was wearing a stunning, deep navy, floor-length robe that was intricately embroidered with flowers of gold. Around her throat was a gold choker and set in it was a huge ruby.

She was simply the most stunning woman Adele had ever seen.

'I am to meet with Zahir…' she said to Adele. 'Can you tell him that I am here?'

Adele would usually ask who it was that wanted to speak with him but there was something so regal about her that she felt it would be rude to do so. As well as that, she had heard Zahir asking Phillip to cover him for a couple of hours as he and Dakan were taking their mother out for afternoon tea.

This was surely his mother—the Queen.

'I'll just let him know.'

There was only Zahir in the nurses' station now. He was still on the computer but just signing off. 'Zahir,' Adele said.

'Yes?' He didn't turn around.

'There's a lady here to see you. I think that it might be your mother.'

'Thank you,' he stood. 'I shall take her around to my office. When Dakan comes, would you tell him where we are?'

'Actually…' Adele halted him. 'I was just coming in to tell you that Mr Richards's blood pressure and heart rate are raised.'

'Does he have pain?'

'He says not, he just wants to sleep.'

'Okay.' Zahir glanced at the chart she held out to him. 'Could you take my mother to my office and have her wait there?'

'Of course,' Adele said. 'What do I call her?'

'I answer to Leila!'

Adele turned and saw that Zahir's mother had followed her into the nurses' station. 'I apologise.' Adele smiled. 'Let me take you through...'

They walked through the department. Leila said how lovely it felt to be in London and to be able to go out with her sons for tea. 'Things are far less formal here than they are back home,' she explained. 'I prefer not to use my title when I am here as people tend to stare.'

They would stare anyway, Adele thought. Leila was seriously beautiful and it was as if she glided rather than walked alongside her.

'I thought you'd have bodyguards,' Adele said, and Leila gave a little laugh.

'My driver is trained as one but he is waiting

outside. I don't need bodyguards when I have my sons close by.'

'Zahir's office is a little tucked away…' Adele explained as they walked through the observation ward, but then she frowned as she realised that the Queen was no longer walking beside her.

She turned around and saw that she was standing and had her fingers pressed into her forehead.

'Are you okay?' Adele checked.

'I'm just a bit…' Leila didn't finish. Instead she drew in a deep breath and Adele could see that she was terribly pale. 'Could you show me where the restroom is?'

'It's there,' Adele said, and pointed her to the staff restroom. 'I'll just wait here for you, shall I?'

Leila nodded and walked off and Adele waited for her to come out.

And waited.

Perhaps she was topping up her make-up, Adele decided, but then she thought about how pale Leila had suddenly gone and Adele was certain that she had been feeling dizzy.

She was loath to interrupt her. After all, Leila was Zahir's mother and she was also a queen.

But, at the end of the day, she was a woman and Adele a nurse and she was starting to become concerned.

Nursing instinct won.

She pushed open the door and stepped in but there was no Leila at the sink washing her hands or doing her make-up. 'Leila?' Adele called into the silence.

'Please help me…' Leila's voice came from behind the cubicle door.

'It's okay, I'm here.' Adele took out the coin that she kept in her pocket for such times. She turned it in the slot and pushed open the door, relieved that it gave and that Leila wasn't leaning against it, as had happened to Adele in the past.

'Don't let my sons see me bleed,' Leila begged.

'I shan't.'

She was bleeding and on the edge of passing out.

'Put your head down,' Adele told her. 'Has this happened before?'

'A couple of times. I am seeing a doctor on Harley Street.'

Adele didn't want to leave her sitting up in case she passed out, but neither did she want to lie her on the floor. She opened the main door to the rest room, at the same time as keeping an eye on her. She saw Janet bringing a patient into the obs ward.

'Janet!' Adele called out in a voice that made the other woman turn around immediately. As she did so Adele ducked straight back into the cubicle, knowing that Janet would follow her in.

'Just take some nice big breaths,' Adele said to Leila.

As Janet entered, Adele brought her up to speed.

'This is Leila, Zahir's mother. She's bleeding PV.'

'I'll go and get a gurney.'

'Janet,' Adele added, before she dashed off, 'she doesn't want Zahir to see.'

It was all swiftly dealt with. Leila was put onto a gurney and oxygen given. Adele put some blankets over her to make sure that she was covered before they wheeled her through.

Of course Zahir had finished with Mr Richards and was making his way to his office as they passed by.

'What happened?' he asked and then he gave a look at Adele as if to say, *I left her with you for five minutes!*

'Your mother fainted,' Adele told him as they walked quickly into the department.

'Maria,' Janet called out to the female registrar who was on duty today.

'I will take care of my mother,' Zahir said as they arrived at the cubicle.

He started to walk in but Adele blocked his path.

Well, she hardly blocked it, because she was very slight and he could easily have moved her aside or stepped around her, but there was something in her stance that was a challenge. 'Zahir!' Adele said, and she looked up at him and, for only the second time in twelve months of their history, their eyes met properly.

'Adele, let me past.'

'No,' she said, and stood her ground. 'Zahir, there are some things a mother would prefer her son didn't see.'

As realisation hit he gave a small nod. 'Very well.'

'We've got this,' Adele reassured him.

He was like a cat put out in the rain but reluctantly he stepped back. 'Could you keep me informed?'

She nodded.

Poor Leila, Adele thought as she got her into a gown and did some obs. Leila point blank refused to allow Adele to remove her jewellery.

Janet inserted an IV and Maria ordered some IV fluids. In a short space of time Zahir's mother was starting to look better.

'I've been unwell for a while,' she explained. 'I came over last month to have some time with my sons but I also had some tests done. I'm supposed to be having a hysterectomy tomorrow. I don't want my husband to know.' She took a breath. 'As awkward as it might be, I was going to tell my sons today at afternoon tea.'

Maria went through her medical history but at first Leila was very vague in her responses.

'How many pregnancies have you had?' Maria asked.

'I have two children.'

'How many pregnancies?' Maria asked again.

'Three,' Leila said, and Adele saw a tear slip from her eyes and into her hair. 'I don't like to speak of that time.'

Maria looked at Adele, whose hand Leila was holding, in the hope Adele could get more out of her. 'The doctor needs to know your history, Leila. She needs to know about your pregnancies and labours and any problems you have had.'

'My womb causes me many problems. I got pregnant very quickly with Zahir but he was born prematurely. It was a very difficult labour.'

They waited for her to elaborate but she didn't.

'And the next pregnancy?' Adele prompted.

'It took five more years to get pregnant and then I had Dakan. Again it was very difficult, he had very large shoulders. Two years later, I was lucky and I fell pregnant but my body did not do well… I had the best healer and a specialist *attar* but there was little they could do for me.'

'*Attar*?' Adele checked.

'He makes up the herbs the healer advises. I took the potion every day yet I still felt very unwell, and I started to vomit.'

'At what stage of the pregnancy?' Maria asked.

'He said I had four months left to go,' Leila answered. 'I was getting worse and I insisted that I be flown to a medical facility overseas. My husband and the healer were very opposed to the idea but I demanded it. In Dubai they said that I had to deliver the baby and that my blood pressure was very high. I called my husband and he said the healer had told him it was too soon and that the baby would die and that I needed to come home. Fatiq flew to Dubai to come and bring me back home…'

Leila started to cry in earnest then. 'But by then I had delivered and the healer was right. A few hours after my husband arrived our son died.'

'I'm so sorry,' Adele said.

'I have a picture of him.'

Adele got Leila's bag and watched as she took out her purse and showed them the tiniest most beautiful baby. 'We named him Aafaq, it means the place where the earth and sky meet.'

'It's a beautiful name,' Adele said, and she looked at a younger Leila and a man who looked very much like Zahir and was probably around the age his son was now.

They were both holding their tiny baby and he was off machines.

'What a beautiful baby,' Adele said.

They were a beautiful family, Adele thought, despite the pain. The King's arm was around his wife and he was gazing down at his son and you could see the love and sorrow in his expression.

'We cannot even speak of Aafaq,' Leila sighed. 'There is too much hurt there to even discuss that time. I think that my husband blames me for turning my back on the healer and yet he loves me also. I want for us to be able to speak about the son we lost but we can't. Aafaq would have been twenty-five years old next month and time still hasn't healed it. I miss him every day.'

It was so sad, Adele thought, and she continued to hold the older woman's hand as Maria examined her. A while later an ultrasound confirmed fibroids and Maria went through the options.

'We have a private wing here and I can speak with the consultant gynaecologist, Mr Oman. Or you can be transferred to the hospital you're already booked into, though I doubt they'd operate tomorrow. You might need a few days to rest and recover from this bleeding.'

'I think I would rather stay here but I shall discuss it with my son. Will you speak with him, please?' Leila asked Maria. 'He will be so worried and I am so embarrassed.'

'Stop thinking like that,' Adele told her. 'Zahir is a doctor, he deals with this sort of thing all the time.'

'Adele's right,' Maria said. 'Can I tell Zahir that you were already planning to have surgery?'

'Yes.' Leila nodded. 'But please don't mention what I said about Aafaq.'

'I shan't. Do you want him to come in when I've finished speaking with him?'

'Please.'

'Check first, though,' Adele called, as Maria left. 'I'm just going to help Leila freshen up.'

Adele left to make preparations so that she could give Leila a wash and change of sheets. When she came back into the cubicle Leila was staring at the photo but then she placed it back in her bag.

It must be so hard for her, Adele thought, not to be able to speak of her son. She wondered if Zahir even knew about the baby his mother had lost.

'Were you going to tell your husband after the operation?' Adele asked as she washed her.

'Yes,' Leila said. 'I might even have told him before or got one of my sons to. I know it is hard to understand our ways,' Leila said. 'Most of the time I am very grateful for the care I receive. There are times, though, that more is needed.'

Aafaq had been one of those times, Adele guessed.

Soon she was washed and changed.

'Thank you for caring for me,' Leila said.

'It's my pleasure. I'm just going to take your blood pressure again.'

She was doing just that when Maria checked that Leila was ready to receive visitors and a concerned-looking Zahir and Dakan came in.

They came over and Zahir gave his mother a warm embrace and spoke kindly to her in Arabic.

'It's okay,' he said. 'You could have told me that you have not been well.'

'I have been trying to deal with it myself.'

'Well, you don't have to. You have two sons who are doctors.'

'The healer seems to think…'

What was being said, Adele did not know but she watched as Zahir's jaw gritted.

'Zahir, don't just dismiss it out of hand. The potion helped at first but in the end was not working. It was the same when…' She didn't finish.

Zahir looked down at his mother's swollen eyes and he knew that she would have been asked about previous pregnancies.

And he knew that subject must not be raised by him.

'When things were getting no better, the healer suggested that when I was in London perhaps I could see someone.'

Zahir frowned. 'He suggested it?'

'Yes,' Leila said, 'but please don't tell your father that. I don't want the healer to get in trouble.'

It was a long afternoon that stretched into the evening. Dakan got paged to go to the ward and Zahir saw patients while keeping an eye on his mother.

Mr Oman came and saw Leila. It was decided that she would be admitted to the private wing and that surgery would take place on Monday.

'For now we'll have you moved somewhere more comfortable and you can get some rest.'

He spoke with Zahir on his way out. 'You know that I shall take the very best care of her.'

'I do. Thank you.'

'Try not to worry. It will be a laparoscopic procedure and there will be minimal downtime.' Mr Oman said.

Zahir knew that.

It was a straightforward operation that his mother had had to travel for ten hours to get access to.

Dakan came in to visit again and they persuaded their mother that Fatiq, the King, needed to be informed as to all that had happened today, and finally she agreed.

'Go easy on him, Zahir,' Leila said, for she knew how they clashed, especially on topics such as this. 'He will be so worried and scared for me.'

Zahir nodded.

And at the beginning of the call, knowing how deeply his parents loved each other and the shock this would be, he was gentle. He sat in his office, explaining as best he could what had happened and that his mother would have surgery on Monday.

'No,' his father said and Zahir could hear the fear in his voice. 'I want her here. Last time she went into hospital…' He didn't finish.

They never did.

That topic was closed for ever.

'Zahir, if anything should happen to her—'

'She needs surgery,' Zahir interrupted, but they went around in circles for a while, with Fatiq insisting that surgery was unnecessary and that the healer could sort this.

Zahir bit back the temptation to tell his father that the healer had been the one who had suggested it.

That had surprised Zahir, yet it pleased him also.

Perhaps some progress could finally be made.

'She is seeing one of the top surgeons in London,' Zahir said. 'I will ensure that she gets the very best of care and shall keep you informed.'

The call ended and Zahir replaced the receiver. He squeezed the bridge of his nose between finger and thumb and took a deep breath to steady himself. He was so angry with his father about the health care back home and it was a battle they had fought for way more than a decade.

It was the reason he was here.

CHAPTER THREE

'ARE YOU OKAY?'

Her voice was soothing.

Pleasant.

He opened his eyes and there, standing at the office door, was Adele.

Zahir thought he had closed it and was uncomfortable that she'd caught him in an unguarded moment.

'I'm not about to have my second Al Rahal faint on me today?' Adele checked, and Zahir gave a reluctant smile.

'No.'

'We're just about to move your mother to the private wing.'

'Good,' Zahir said, and then glanced at the time. 'You must be finishing up. Thank you for all your help with her today.'

'You're welcome.'

'Who's taking her up to the ward?'

'I am,' Adele said.

His mother had insisted on keeping Adele around and, because queens were something of a rarity, the rules had been relaxed.

'She wants to know if you've spoken with her husband.'

'Tell my mother that he knows. I'll come and speak with her on the ward. I just have a couple more patients to see.'

It took ages to settle Leila into the private wing. She was lovely but extremely demanding and by the time Adele had everything to the Queen's liking and had handed over it was way past the end of her shift and she was exhausted.

'I shall see you in the morning,' Leila checked as Adele wished her goodnight.

Zahir had come in to check that his mother was settled too.

'No.' Adele shook her head.

'But you said you started tomorrow at seven.'

'Yes, but I work in Emergency.'

There was an exchange in Arabic between mother and son. A rather long one and finally Zahir translated what was being said.

'She wants to know if you can nurse her. I've just explained that that is not how things work.'

Leila spoke now in English. 'I want Adele to be my nurse.'

'She's very used to getting her own way.' Zahir gave a wry smile and then went back to speaking in Arabic.

His mother was adamant and, seeing that she was getting upset, Adele intervened.

'Leila, I would love to care for you but it isn't my specialty and I'm already rostered on to work in Accident and Emergency tomorrow. They're very short of staff. I can come and visit you, though.'

'You'll visit me?'

'I'd love to.' Adele nodded. She often caught up with patients once they were moved to other wards and few were more interesting than Leila. 'I can come in during my lunch break tomorrow.

For now, though, you need to get some rest. It's been an exhausting day for you.'

Adele headed down and changed out of her scrubs and into jeans and a T-shirt. It was well after ten and she had missed her bus and would have to wait for ages for the next one.

It wasn't the first time it had happened and it certainly wouldn't be the last.

It was, however, the first time that the silver sports car that usually glided past pulled in at the bus stop.

The window slid down and Zahir called out to her.

'The least I can do is give you a lift home.'

Even though Adele was still sulking about last night, she knew it would be petty to refuse.

Finally she sat in the passenger seat.

'You don't drive?' Zahir asked.

'No.' Adele shook her head. 'There's no real need to in London.'

She gave her regular excuse, but the truth was that since that awful day even the thought of getting behind the wheel made her feel ill.

'Surely it's better than getting a bus late at night?'

'Maybe.' Adele gave a shrug.

Perhaps she couldn't afford a car, Zahir thought. He had heard that she was saving up to move out of her flat.

He would buy her a car, Zahir decided.

It was as if cultures had just clashed in his brain.

That was what his family would say—buy her a car, repay the debt, return the favour tenfold—and yet he knew that she would find such a move offensive.

Today was not a debt that needed to be repaid to Adele.

It was her job. Nursing was what she did.

And she did it very well.

It wasn't her fault that he was terse with her at times.

It was necessary for him to function.

She entranced him.

She was funny and open and yet private and deep.

Adele was the woman he kept a distance from

because she was the one person he would really like to get to know.

And no good could come from that.

'I really am grateful for all your help today,' he said.

'I was just doing my job.'

'I know, but you helped my mother a lot. I know that she would have been scared, given that she is so far from home, and that she would have needed someone to talk to.' Zahir hesitated. He thought of his mother's eyelids, swollen from crying. He hoped she had given her full history to the doctors. 'Did she mention that she lost a baby?'

Adele frowned as Zahir glanced at her. From the way Leila had asked that it not be mentioned, Adele had assumed Zahir didn't know about his brother. She thought about it some more and realised he would have been about seven when it had happened.

When she didn't answer the question, Zahir elaborated.

'I don't really know the details,' he admitted. 'It's a forbidden subject in the palace. I just know she was having a baby and that she flew to Dubai. Then my father left and they all returned. Aafaq is buried in the desert but to this day…' He glanced at her again, hoping he might glean something.

Anything.

'You need to discuss that with your mother,' Adele said, though there was regret in her voice. She knew how it felt to be kept in the dark. She could still clearly remember trying to get information out of Janet. It was awful knowing someone held facts that were vital to you but could not be shared. 'I'm sorry.'

'I know,' Zahir admitted. 'And I'm sorry to have put you in that situation. I just hope she has been frank with Mr Oman.'

Adele didn't answer.

Zahir respected her for that.

'Just here,' Adele said, and they pulled up at a large building with heavy gates.

'Again—thank you again for your help with my mother today.'

'No problem. Thank you for the lift.'

'Any time.' Zahir gave an automatic response.

She let out a short, incredulous laugh. For a year he had driven past her; last night she had been drenched and he'd utterly ignored her. And, yes, it might seem petty but she would not leave it unsaid. 'Any time you feel *obliged* to, you mean.'

Zahir stared ahead but he was gripping the steering-wheel rather tightly.

He knew that Adele was referring to last night.

Of course he had seen her.

It had taken all he had not to stop.

'Goodnight, Zahir.'

She got out and opened the gates.

Zahir knew he hadn't dropped her at her flat. This was a nursing home. He knew that Adele's mother was very ill and that she visited her often.

He had never delved.

Zahir had wanted to, though.

He wanted to explore his feelings for Adele. He wanted her more than he had ever wanted anyone.

But he had been born to be king, which meant at all times he kept his head. His emotions he owned and his heart had to remain closed until marriage.

And he would marry soon hopefully.

It was the last bargaining tool he had with his father.

King Fatiq wanted a selection ceremony to take place and for Zahir to choose his future bride.

There were several possibilities and the union must be the one to best benefit the country, yet Zahir had refused to commit himself so far.

Only when he had free rein to rebuild the health system in his own country would Zahir choose a bride. His father had resisted but Zahir was now thirty-two and the King wanted his son married and home.

And so Zahir chose to remain aloof in relationships, knowing, hoping, that at any given time his father might relent and summon him home and the work on the health system in his country could truly begin.

There was nothing aloof about his feelings for Adele, though.

It could only prove perilous to get involved with her.

The last time he had been home he had sat in the desert and asked for a solution.

Always he asked for help regarding Aafaq and the clash with his father, and always he asked how best to serve his people. Lately, he had asked about Adele.

There could be no solution there, Zahir knew.

Yet he had asked for guidance and in the quiet of deep meditation the answer had been the same.

Have patience.

In time the answers will unfold.

Do what is essential.

Zahir's patience was running out.

He watched as Adele pressed the buzzer and then she turned around and frowned.

She was surprised that the man who left her standing in the dark night after night seemed to want to see her safely inside.

Within a matter of moments she was walking into the nursing home and towards her mother's room.

'Hi, Adele.' Annie, one of the nurses, had just

finished turning her mother and smiled at Adele as she came in.

'I know that it's late but I couldn't get here this morning and…'

Adele stopped herself. They always told her that she didn't need to give a reason if she couldn't come in. Tomorrow she wouldn't be able to—she was on an early shift and, even though the nursing home was close by, she was going out on that date with Paul.

The trouble was she wasn't particularly looking forward to it.

'Hi, Mum,' Adele said, and took a seat and held one of her mother's hands.

Lorna's nails were painted a lovely shade of coral.Adele did her mother's finger- and toenails each week. Her once brown hair was now a silver grey. Adele had used to faithfully do her roots but in the end she had stopped that.

Oh, she knew she had to get a life and yet it was so hard not to come in and visit.

And people simply didn't understand.

Lorna had been so vibrant and outgoing. A single mum, she had juggled work and her daughter, along with an active social life. She'd had a large group of friends and at first they, along with relatives, had filled the ICU waiting rooms and then later they had come by to visit when Lorna had been on the ward.

Over the years those visits had all but petered out.

Now the occasional card or letter came and Adele would read it out then add it to the string on her mother's wall. Lorna's sister, Adele's aunt, came and visited maybe once or twice a year. Another friend dropped in on occasion but apart from that it was just Adele.

And so she brought her mother, who lay with her eyes closed, up to date on what was happening in her life.

'I finally my got my lift from him,' Adele told her mum. 'It was very underwhelming.' It really had been, she thought. 'Anyway, I'm over Zahir. I really do mean it this time. I'm going out with Paul tomorrow night. He's one of the paramedics,' Adele explained to the silence. 'He's asked me out a few times and I decided maybe I should give him a chance after all. I guess I'm not going to like everyone in the same way I do Zahir.'

It really was time to get a life.

But then she told her mother the real reason she had stopped by after work.

It wasn't just that she might not be in tomorrow, there were bigger reasons than that for her being here tonight.

If her mother would just squeeze her hand or blink or do one thing to acknowledge that she knew Adele was here, it would help.

This was agony, it truly was, sitting here day in, day out, and yet she was all her mother had.

But Adele made herself say it out loud.

'Mum, I've got some annual leave that I need to take and I'm thinking of going on holiday.'

It was a huge thing for her to say.

Yet she knew she couldn't live this life for ever.

To pay for the nursing home and the legal fees when the other family involved in the accident had sued, the family home had been sold and

Adele now shared a small flat with Helga and James.

Adele had deferred her studies for two years, but they had been spent dealing with the aftermath of the accident. She hadn't had a holiday in years. Any weekends or leave had always been taken up with other things, such as university, work, visiting her mother, getting the house ready for the market or dealing with lawyers, doctors and real estate agents.

Finally, when her mum had been placed in this home and things had started to settle, Adele had started her role in Accident and Emergency.

Now she felt as if she was coming up for air and she simply wanted to get away and maybe just grieve for her mother.

Of course she would still visit, Adele thought as she walked the small distance home to her flat.

But she had to work out some sort of balance.

Helga was in the kitchen, making an enormous fry-up for herself and James, and she had her music up loud.

Adele was so tired but she lay on her bed, try-

ing not to think of what she had just told her
mother and trying to consider where to go on
holiday.

Greece perhaps?

She woke to that thought.

Adele took out her laptop and looked at several
destinations and then saw a wonderful package
deal for the South of France.

Oh!

It was more expensive than she had planned for.

Then again, she hadn't really planned to be
going away.

Walking towards the bus stop, she saw that a
one-bedroom flat nearby had just come up for
rent.

Perhaps the money would be better spent moving out than on two weeks overseas.

Arriving at work, she smiled at Janet, who was
waiting for the rest of the early-shift staff to arrive before they had handover, which wouldn't
take long, given that the place appeared dead.

Zahir was sitting on hold on the phone and not
looking in the sunniest of moods.

'How's the holiday planning going?' Janet asked as Adele came over.

'I've seen something nice for the South of France.'

'Ooh, la la,' Helene said as she joined the group. 'Will you go topless?'

'I might.' Adele said. 'And I might find myself a nice French man…'

'What about Paul?' Janet checked.

'Oh, yes.' Adele said, her voice a touch deflated.

'You've got your hot date tonight!' Janet reminded her, and Adele rolled her eyes. 'Where's he taking you?'

'No idea.' Adele shrugged.

Zahir tried to ignore the conversation. Adele was going out on a date, well, of course she was.

She was beautiful, seriously so, and it had nothing to do with him what she did in her free time.

But this wasn't her free time.

'Is it appropriate,' Zahir said tartly as he hung up the phone, 'to be discussing topless bathing and dating in a corridor.'

'Er, Zahir.' Janet, who knew a thing or three, and had been enjoying winding him up, answered with her own version of tartness. 'There are absolutely no patients around. I can handle my nursing staff, thank you.'

She smiled as Zahir stalked off.

Oh, yes.

She knew full well that he liked Adele.

CHAPTER FOUR

IT WAS A busy morning and lunchtime soon came around. Adele made good on her promise to visit Leila.

'You are looking so much better.' Adele was delighted to see the other woman sitting up and that she had some colour in her cheeks. Her hair was up and, despite wearing a hospital gown, she looked amazing.

'I am feeling it,' Leila agreed. 'Thank you for all your help yesterday. Honestly, I shudder to think what might have happened. We could have been at afternoon tea!'

'Don't think like that.' Adele smiled.

'It's hard not to,' Leila sighed. 'There's not much else to do here. It is so nice to have you come and see me. I am used to being very busy. To just lie in bed is so frustrating. Zahir and

Dakan have been in, of course, and the nurses here are very kind, but I am so bored.'

'Will your husband come and visit you now that he knows you're having surgery?'

'No.' Leila shook her head. 'He does not like hospitals.'

It must be lonely for her, Adele thought.

'He was going to send one of my handmaids but I have told him not to. I have asked Dakan to bring my embroidery from the hotel. That will take my mind off things.'

Leila was so easy to talk to. She was the complete opposite of Zahir, who, Adele guessed from the little she had gleaned, took after his father. Leila was more open and outgoing, rather like Dakan.

'So you have days off this weekend?' Leila asked.

'I do.' Adele nodded. 'Then I'm on night duty for a fortnight.'

'They must be tiring,' Leila said, and then looked at Adele and saw the smudges under her eyes and her pale features. 'Though you look tired now, even before you have started your night duty.'

'I am tired,' Adele admitted, and not just to Leila but to herself. It had been an exhausting few years and Janet was right to insist that she take her leave. 'I've got a holiday coming up.'

'That's exciting. Are you going anywhere nice?'

'I haven't decided yet. I'll have a think about it this weekend.'

As they chatted Adele revealed that she was going on a date that evening.

'A first date.' Leila beamed.

'I'm actually not looking forward to it,' Adele admitted. 'I'm thinking of cancelling but I can't come up with a good enough excuse.'

'What do your parents think of him?' Leila asked.

'They...' Adele paused. 'I think your idea of a first date and mine are a little bit different, we're just going out for dinner.'

'Oh, yes.' Leila nodded. 'I sometimes forget. By the time I had my first date with Fatiq he was already my husband.' She laughed.

'Had you met him before you married?'

'Yes, there was a selection ceremony two months before the wedding. I knew though that I would be chosen. Or rather I hoped. From when I was a little girl I always knew who I would marry. I told him that I came with conditions, though,' Leila said, and tapped the ruby at her throat.

Adele guessed Leila meant she had told Fatiq that she must be kept in splendour.

'Well, I can't see myself ever marrying Paul,' Adele admitted. 'I can't even picture getting through dinner.'

'Your parents haven't met him, then?'

'No.' Adele shook her head. 'My parents divorced when I was very young and my father has never had anything to do with me.'

'And your mother?'

'She was in an accident,' Adele said. 'She's very unwell and is in a nursing home. I see her every day.'

'And you're visiting me too!'

'No, I *like* visiting you,' she said, and then closed her eyes on the sudden threat of tears.

Adele never cried but she was suddenly close to it now as she had practically admitted the truth—she didn't like visiting her mum.

Leila's hand went over hers.

It was unexpected and also terribly kind, given what she had just said.

'She can't talk or react,' Adele told Leila. 'She's just a shell of herself. I don't even think she knows that I'm there.'

'You know that you're there for her, though,' Leila said. 'That's the important thing.'

Finally, someone who understood, Adele thought.

Her family, friends and colleagues all encouraged her to step back. Even the nursing staff at the home gently implied that Adele didn't need to visit quite so much.

Adele knew that she had to sort out her life—she didn't need to be told that but it was so nice to have someone understand.

'I'm worried about going on holiday,' she admitted.

'Can I tell you something?' Leila offered. 'I want to have a holiday. I love my country and my people but because of certain ways...' She hesitated and then explained. 'Always there must be a royal in residence. Fatiq was already a king when we married so I never even had a honeymoon. Now one of my sons steps in if we have to go away for formal occasions. Usually it is Zahir, but both of them have busy lives, so they only return when they must. I know that a holiday would be rejuvenating. I dream of having some time away with my husband to replenish myself, although I can't see it ever happening. Take some time for yourself, Adele, and you will return refreshed and better able to take care of your mother.'

It helped to hear that.

The wise, gentle words made Adele feel better about taking a short break.

'I must get back to work.' It had been nice talking and before she went Adele wished Leila well for her operation on Monday.

'I doubt you'll be up to visitors on Monday night but I'll come in after my shift on Tuesday morning.'

'I shall look forward to it,' Leila said. 'Enjoy dinner tonight.'

Adele did.

Her date went well, in fact. Paul was nice, and perfectly fine, except she didn't fancy him.

Not a bit.

And it neither started nor ended with a kiss.

It just wasn't there.

For Adele at least.

Monday came and in the afternoon Adele lay in bed, trying to get some sleep before her night shift.

Then Helga and James started to row.

Again.

She had gone to look at the one-bedroom flat, along with many others. She had put an application in and all Adele could do now was hope.

Oh, Leila was right, she needed a break.

She had two weeks of night duty to get through and then the world was her oyster.

Not quite.

She sat up and reached for her laptop and checked her bank account.

Still, it didn't stop her from daydreaming. She liked the look of Greece though she was still considering the South of France when an advert for exotic honeymoon destinations caught her eye.

Well, not the honeymoon word. Adele couldn't even get the excitement up for a second date. Paul had called over the weekend, suggesting that they go to the movies, but she had said no.

There was no point.

No, it was the destination that had her pause.

Mamlakat Almas.

That was where Zahir was from.

Adele clicked on it and immediately she was swept away.

She found out that the name translated to Kingdom of Diamonds.

It looked incredible. Adele watched a short film. It was taken from the air and she saw the azure water and the pristine white beaches. From snatches of conversations when she had worked with Dakan and from the odd comment Zahir had made, she had thought it was all ancient buildings and desert. And, yes, there was all of that—the film led her through the desert and she saw a caravan of camels and Bedouin tribes as well as colourful souqs. The city skyline, though, was modern, with golden high-rise buildings that shimmered in the sun.

And there, most beautiful of all, was Qasr Almas.

Diamond Palace.

Zahir's home.

It was spectacular—an imposing white residence with beach and ocean on the one side yet the desert started directly behind and spread into the distance.

The palace was dotted with stones, rubies, emeralds, and sapphires and some diamonds too.

Adele wanted to see it and she wanted to be there in the souqs and especially out in the desert.

She read the comments and most agreed it

was an amazing destination. There was a certain magic to it, many said, and it was perfect for a honeymoon or romantic getaway.

Then Adele read the negative comments and they were all pretty much the same.

Don't get taken ill there!
Bring your own medication!

And one was aimed at a tour guide.

He couldn't even answer why the palace is called Diamond Palace and yet it is mainly coloured stones.

Oh, she would love to go there.

Right now, though, she needed to sleep.

It was bad enough trying to sleep when she was working days—her flatmates liked to party hard, it didn't matter what day of the week. Trying to sleep during the day was almost impossible—there were doors slamming, arguments breaking out. After a fitful sleep Adele woke to the sound of the television blaring and loud chatter from the kitchen as supper was being made.

She was tired before her shift even started. It was going to be a very long night.

Zahir also wasn't having the best of days.

While he was grateful that his mother's operation had gone smoothly, he was furious that it had to come to this.

There was only one small hospital in his home town. Zahir had had several architects working on plans for a new one, yet his father had halted him every step of the way and in the end the project had been abandoned.

The whole health system in Mamlakat Almas needed to be addressed and better ways implemented.

The main reason that Zahir and his brother had chosen to study medicine had been so that they could knowledgeably implement the changes that were needed, yet they were thwarted at every turn. Their father refused to move forward and over and over he came up with reasons why the plans for the hospital could not go ahead.

Zahir had now had enough.

Finding out that his mother had had to travel to another country just to get suitable treatment did not sit well with him.

He looked at his mother, drowsy from anaesthetic, and was told by Mr Oman that surgery had gone well. 'I'm surprised she waited so long,' the surgeon commented.

Zahir was sure his mother had been struggling for a long time and it meant his mood was not the most pleasant as he made his way back to the emergency department after visiting her.

And Zahir's already dark mood did not improve when he saw a woman holding a large bouquet of flowers asking one of the nurses if they could be delivered to Adele Jenson.

'She's not on duty till tonight,' the nurse said, taking the flower arrangement. 'But I'll see that she gets them.'

Once the delivery woman had gone a debate took place as to who had sent the flowers.

'She had a date with Paul on Friday,' someone said.

Zahir did not want to think about that but the flowers seemed to follow him everywhere.

They were in the nurses' station as he wrote his notes. And when, having checked on his mother again in the late afternoon, he went to make a drink, someone had moved them through to the staff kitchen.

He went to his office to make a call to his father.

The King.

He sat at the desk for a long moment, thinking hard. There was a lot on his mind. Admin were demanding his signature on a new contract, as they had every right to do.

Zahir knew, though, that he needed to go home and not just for a visit this time.

He was thinking of going head to head with his father so that he could get the hospital under way.

There was another reason, though, that he hadn't signed his new contract—Adele.

The attraction had been instant and troublesome. He could still vividly remember the first time he'd laid eyes on her. Working on a patient, usually nothing could have drawn his attention, yet for a fleeting moment she had.

Her china-blue eyes had met his and Janet had explained that Adele was there for an interview.

He hadn't wanted her to get the job.

That was how much he was attracted to her. Even before they had spoken, he would have preferred that they never had. Of course she had been given the role and two weeks later he had walked into the nurses' station to the sound of her laughter and her fresh fragrance.

'Zahir,' Janet had said. 'This is Adele. She is a graduate nurse...'

'Adele.' He had responded with a brief nod.

'Hi!' She had smiled.

'Adele did her training here,' Janet had explained, 'so she's familiar with the place.'

Zahir had shut her out at every possibility. He'd asked for more senior staff when possible. He'd ignored her slightly wacky humour and had not rewarded it with a smile.

He'd dated sophisticated beauties and he'd told

them upfront that he was in no position to settle down.

Currently he was dating Bella.

That was about to end and he knew Bella sensed it. He had used the excuse of his mother being sick this weekend not to see her and now she had come up with tickets to the theatre next week.

He would end it before then.

Soon he would marry a bride considered suitable.

Of course he would be consulted, but the effect of her laughter on the edge of his lips would not be taken into consideration. Neither would the fact that the mere scent of her made him want to turn around.

There would be a more logical thought process when it came to the selection of the future Queen. Perhaps her country would have a considerable army, for it would be a marriage of countries rather than hearts. Of course Zahir was not considering Adele for such a role. Yet, on sight, his guard had gone up and he'd known he'd have to be wary of the attraction he felt.

It was an attraction so intense that over the last year every time he had driven past her at the bus stop he had wanted to slow down and tell her to get in. Not to take her home but to take her to his bed.

To make slow, tender love to her.

Yes, he had slowed down the car once, but the sight of her in that short wet dress had been too much.

She was a relentless assault to his senses and six feet three of turned-on sheikh had decided it was safer to drive on.

It was hell to drive past her and leave her standing in the dark. It was hell to work alongside her.

It was hell.

And perhaps time away was needed before self-control ran out.

Nothing could come of them, Zahir knew that. It was the reason that he kept his distance.

His feelings for Adele were serious and that was why he held well and truly back. But it was getting harder to do so.

And it was another reason why it might be better to return to his country.

Zahir rang home.

'I have just come from visiting the Queen.' Zahir spoke formally with his father. 'She is doing very well.'

'How long until she can come home?' The King asked.

'Not until she is ready,' Zahir said. 'I have spoken with Mr Oman and usually it would be several weeks before she could fly but, given she will be on the royal jet, I don't expect it to be that long. And I shall accompany her, of course.' He took a breath and then told his father what he had decided. 'I am not renewing my contract at the hospital. I'm coming home to sort out the building of the new hospital. I'm going to be speaking with architects over the coming weeks. I shall do my best to find someone who can understand the need to respect our traditions, as well as incorporate the new. When I return things will immediately get under way.'

'Nothing is to get under way without my permission.'

'Too many lives have been lost,' Zahir said. 'Your delay in implementing changes has caused your own wife to collapse. What about all our people?'

'I am King.'

'And I am Crown Prince and I refuse to do nothing until your death. I shall be returning with the Queen and change will happen.'

'Don't speak of this now, Zahir. Not when I am concerned for my wife—'

'No,' Zahir interrupted. 'You can no longer ignore that fact that there are better ways. The Queen collapsed while she was visiting me at work. What if she had been at a formal dinner or a royal event? Luckily she was in a hospital at the time.'

Zahir let out a tense breath, embarrassed on behalf of his mother as to how events could have panned out.

He was so grateful that Adele had dealt with things so discreetly.

Adele.

All roads led to her.

Even in the middle of a difficult conversation he smiled at the memory of her blocking his path as he had tried to get into the cubicle to care for his mother.

Then his smile faded and he returned to the subject.

'We shall discuss this in person,' Zahir said to his father. 'For now, know that she is resting comfortably and that she is receiving *excellent* medical care.'

'If you are returning then there shall be a selection ceremony and a wedding.'

'You know where I stand on that,' Zahir said. 'I will not marry and have children when I cannot ensure adequate health care for them.'

Zahir hung up.

He saw a few more patients and then went through to the staffroom. Those flowers really were following him. They had been placed on the table and the word 'Adele' had been written on a sheet of paper, as well as an arrow, a row of hearts and a lot of question marks.

It was tease from the other nurses, informing her that she would need to explain!

Zahir did not want to hear it.

Adele walked into the staffroom fifteen minutes before the start of her shift to the beautiful sight of Zahir stretched out and asleep on a sofa. His mouth was slightly open, he needed to shave, but she'd prefer that he did not. But then her heart sank when she saw the large floral arrangement and the note with her name on it. Not for a second did she hope that the flowers were from Zahir. With trepidation she opened the card and read the message.

Adele
Thanks for a great night. Hope to do it again very soon.
Paul x

Unlike their date, there was a kiss at the end.

Zahir awoke to the sickly scent of flowers and to Adele's blue eyes as she stood in the middle of the staffroom.

She looked over as he stirred and wondered what it would be like to wake up beside him.

'You got flowers.' He stated the obvious.

'I did.'

But not from you, her eyes accused.

Never anything from you.

Not even a smile.

'How is your mother?'

'She's doing well.' Zahir stretched his long body. 'The operation went smoothly.'

'That's good.' she said, wondering how the mere sight of him stretching had her on slow burn. How a night being wined and dined by a friendly and good-looking Paul couldn't garner a kiss, yet she could happily go over and straddle Zahir right here and right now.

Honestly!

She had never slept with anyone but she could almost feel the pull in her groin to walk over to him, to bend her head and to kiss that sulky mouth.

He sat up and she was very glad that he did.

'My mother said that you have been visiting her and are going to see her again.'

'I just thought with her being so far from home—' Adele started to explain, but Zahir cut in.

'I appreciate it,' he said, and then abruptly stood and left.

It didn't feel as if he appreciated it, Adele thought as he stalked off.

Still, she wasn't visiting Leila to earn favours from him.

She liked his mother and enjoyed their conversations.

Adele missed talking with her mum so much and Leila helped with that.

Zahir went home and it was a quiet night in Emergency, which made it a very long one. By morning, all Adele wanted was to go to sleep but she remembered she had promised to visit Leila.

'Don't forget your flowers,' Janet called out as she left.

Blasted things, Adele thought, but then she decided they might brighten the room up a little for her visitor.

'Flowers!' Leila was wearing a gorgeous night-gown, had all her jewels on and was back to looking stunning. She smiled when Adele knocked on her door and quickly dabbed her eyes with a handkerchief. 'You shouldn't have.'

'I didn't,' Adele admitted. She knew Leila had been crying. 'The man I went out with on Friday sent them.' She rolled her eyes.

'Do tell.'

Adele did.

Well, a little bit.

'It didn't go well.'

'Why?'

Because he wasn't your sexy son!

'It just didn't,' Adele said. 'I kept wanting to check my phone. That's not a good sign, is it?'

Leila laughed.

'Then he called over the weekend and asked me out again and I said no. I thought he'd got the message but he sent these. I didn't want to look like an idiot on the bus, and I thought they might cheer you up.'

'Well, they have.'

They were like a snowflake in a snowstorm, though, Adele thought as she looked around.

There were flowers everywhere.

'How do you feel?' she asked Leila.

'I had a lot of pain in the evening but they changed my pain control and now I feel much more comfortable. I've just had my first drink of tea. I asked Mr Oman when I can go back to the hotel. He says not for a few more days.'

'You've got on your jewels.'

Leila nodded. 'I was appalled when they told me I had to have them off for surgery. I insisted they were brought to Recovery and I was to wake up with them on.'

Adele smiled.

'Adele,' Leila said, 'I've been thinking.'

'About what?'

'Well, I need a private nurse and I would very much like it to be you.'

'I'm on night shift for the next couple of weeks,' Adele said.

'No, I'm not talking about back at the hotel. I mean for you to fly back with me. You said that you wanted a holiday.'

Adele's shocked expression was misinterpreted.

'I wouldn't be making too many demands on you,' Leila said quickly. 'I would just feel safer knowing I had a nurse for those first few days at home, and then you could do what you wanted. I would page you if required. You would have your own wing with its own beach and of course you would be well reimbursed.'

'Leila…' Adele didn't know what to say.

She was stunned to be asked and very flattered too.

And the more she thought about it, the more excited she felt.

There, in her chest, was something that had been missing for so long—the hope of adventure.

The thought of Zahir didn't enter her head. Not at that moment. He would be here, working. This had nothing to do with him.

It was the thought of a holiday at such an exotic location. Yes, it would be a working holiday perhaps but that suited Adele even better—it didn't have to be a holiday *or* a new flat, she could have both.

Yet hope was dashed even before it took form.

'Ah, Zahir!'

Adele, who had been perched on the bed, hurriedly stood up as Leila greeted her son. He was dressed in a suit for now. No doubt later he would be wearing scrubs, but for now he was all glossy and freshly showered, and the scent of his cologne as he came over was more heady than a room full of flowers. 'I was just saying to Leila that I need a private nurse and she had told me that she has some annual leave coming up. I thought—'

'I will arrange your nurse,' Zahir interrupted, and his voice was terse.

'I don't need you to arrange anything,' Leila said. 'I would like Adele—'

'Adele is a junior emergency nurse. I shall find a surgical nurse who specialises in wom-

en's health to take care of you. In fact, I already
have. She will be looking after you when you go
back to the hotel.'

'Zahir!' Leila reprimanded her son.

'It's fine.' Adele halted them. Her cheeks were
on fire and she was angry and hurt at Zahir's
cutting words. Clearly he didn't even think her
capable of nursing what would by then be a two
week post-op patient. 'It was lovely of you to
think of me, Leila… I really do have to go now.'

She said goodbye and gave a very brief nod to
Zahir.

'Zahir,' his mother admonished once they were
alone. 'You were very rude to speak like that in
front of her.'

'I work with Adele.' He shrugged. 'I shall find
a more suitable nurse. Anyway, perhaps *you* were
the one who was rude. Adele might already have
plans.' He tried not to think of her topless on a
beach in France and then he thought of Paul.
'Maybe she wants to go away with her boy-
friend…'

'Rubbish,' Leila said. 'She doesn't have one.

In fact...' She gestured to her locker and those flowers really were following him everywhere because Zahir caught sight of them as Leila continued to speak.

'She had a disastrous date on Friday. She said all she wanted to do was to check her phone. She spends all her spare time taking care of her mother and I want to do something nice for her.'

Zahir held in an exasperated sigh.

There was a debt to be paid and his mother had now come up with a way to pay it.

'I shall think of a more suitable way to thank her,' Zahir said, and then he asked a question. 'Why do you want Adele?'

It was a question he had asked himself many times over the past year.

'I find her easy to talk to and she knows about...' Leila shook her head and lay back on her pillow and closed her eyes. 'It doesn't matter. I'm going to have a little rest now. I've been up since five.'

The subject was closed.

So many subjects were closed.

He could see that she had been crying and Zahir thought about what Adele had said to him in the car: *You need to discuss that with your mother.*

He didn't know how to, though.

He could speak with grief-stricken parents, he could tell someone, with skill and care, that they did not have long to live.

Yet this was a conversation that was almost impossible to start. From seven years old he had been warned not to ask questions. Not to upset his mother or anger his father by bringing the subject of his brother up.

But they weren't at the palace and things had been left unsaid for far too long.

'I miss him too,' Zahir said to his mother, and he watched her face crumple. 'I know I never saw him, but I still think of him and when I go to our desert abode I pray for him each time.'

As Leila started to cry he let her and then after a while she asked him something.

'Could you pass my bag?'

She took out her purse and Zahir saw his

brother for the first time as his mother spoke. As he finally found out what had happened Zahir wasn't in doctor mode, or crown prince mode, he was just remembering the sadness and the silence that had returned with his parents to the palace and he looked at the tiny, beautiful reason why.

'Zahir, I had to tell the doctor about Aafaq and Adele was there when I did so. I don't want to go through it all with another nurse. I am very tearful at the moment. I know that. Mr Oman says it is to be expected after such an operation and it may continue for a few weeks. Maybe the nurse you arranged can care for me at the hotel—'

'You don't need to be in a hotel,' Zahir said. 'Please come back to my home.'

'Your home is in Mamlakat Almas,' Leila told him. 'I would prefer to stay in a hotel.'

Despite being more open than Fatiq, she did not approve of his lifestyle here. Leila did not like the fact that Zahir and Dakan dated when there was an array of brides waiting for them to choose from.

Staying in a hotel was her protest.

'Please let me have Adele care for me.'

'I'll think about it,' he said.

Adele was all he could think about of late.

He had been about to head to Admin to tell them he was taking the last fortnight on his contract as leave and that he would not be renewing it.

The ramifications of a relationship with Adele had long troubled him—his father frowned on his lifestyle here and certainly any serious relationship would be even more frowned upon. It would be dire indeed if anything happened in Mamlakat Almas. He could never choose Adele. The rift it would create between him and his father would be irreparable.

The King was a stickler for tradition and those traditions did not allow for a woman without a title who had dated before.

He could well be exiled and unable to fulfil his duty to his country.

No, he did not want to consider his mother's request.

He was trying to get away from Adele.

Not bring her to his home.

CHAPTER FIVE

FOR A MOMENT there Adele had thought that her luck was finally changing.

You make your own luck, Adele told herself.

She just didn't know how.

It was her second week of nights and she couldn't wait for them to be done and for her two-week break to commence.

She was still smarting at Zahir.

It was six p.m. and there was a staff accreditation that Adele needed to have signed off. She wanted to get it done before she went on annual leave.

She wasn't going to the south of France. Despite the offer still being available, it remained too expensive, so she had decided she would take the Eurotunnel to Paris.

In the morning she would book it.

It really was time to move on with her life, while still including her mother.

And she *was* going to have a holiday romance. Absolutely she was.

She was tired of her lack of a love life and that she was twenty-four years old and still a virgin.

And, as she went over to the nurses' station and Zahir didn't even acknowledge her, she decided was tired of having feelings for someone who thought so little of her.

He looked immaculate. He was wearing his suit and clearly hoped to get away quickly.

'Zahir,' Meg asked, 'is there any chance of you staying back?'

'I can't,' he said. 'I have to finish at six. Bella is waiting for me to pick her up. We are going to the theatre.'

Ouch, Adele thought.

'I just need to write up this drug regime and then I'll have to go,' he said.

With all the drama of his mother being sick and settling her into the hotel, as well as the constant calls back home, he had forgotten to tell Bella they were over. Zahir did not want to put it off for even one more night. He would tell her tonight soon after the curtain came down.

Helene came in then, all ready for staff accreditation too before her night shift.

The staff rotated, and did two weeks of nights every twelve weeks or so.

'You made it!' Janet smiled.

'I nearly didn't.' Helene gave a dramatic sigh. 'I took Hayden out for a driving lesson this afternoon and I've decided I'd rather pay for an instructor. I actually value my life. Honestly, he's—'

'Adele.' Janet halted Helene's latest rant about her son. 'Could you get the annual leave roster from my desk?'

Janet had seen Adele's eyes shutter.

It wasn't Helene's fault. She didn't know.

Few did, but Helene loved to give dramatic blow-by-blow accounts of her day, and with her son just learning to drive, it must be pretty hellish for Adele.

'You know Adele's mother isn't well?' Janet checked with Helene once Adele had gone.

'Yes…'

'She suffered a severe head injury. Adele was at the wheel of the car—she was learning to drive at the time.'

'Oh, no.' Helene cringed. 'I didn't know.'

'Of course you didn't, she doesn't really talk about it. Just know that she's had the most awful time.'

Zahir said nothing.

He finished writing up the chart and headed to his office.

There was Adele coming towards him with the roster.

'Adele…' he said, but she didn't stop walking.

In fact, she brushed past him.

She was on the edge of tears at what Helene had said and she never broke down. Right now, she knew, Janet would be having a discreet word with Helen. And she was fed up too with Zahir. She was tired of smiling only to never have it returned, and being offered the dream job just to have it snatched away by him had been the final straw.

At least she hoped that it was.

She was over him for good.

Oh, no, she would not turn around.

'Enjoy the theatre,' she called over her shoulder, and there was a jealous barb in her tone.

She was cross with him and hurt by him and too weary to not let it show.

Still, she had a fun couple of hours spent with mannequins being signed off on her CPR technique. Having found out she was going to Paris, Janet had remembered a beret she had in her locker and had put it on Ken, the mannequin, when it was Adele's turn.

'Ooh, Ken,' Adele said in a terrible French accent as she knelt over him, 'Why do you just lie there so still? Let's get this heart racing…'

Janet was laughing loudly and then looked up at the open door. 'Oh, Zahir, I thought you'd gone.'

'I'm just leaving now.'

She got more reaction out of Ken, Adele thought as, blushing, she massaged his chest.

The best bit was supper was provided!

Maria came in and grabbed a couple of sandwiches. 'I'm about to go home,' she said. 'Janet I tried not to admit anyone, but I've got a patient that needs to be in the obs ward overnight. Her name is Gladys Williams. She's eighty and had too much to drink and fell and hit her head. I can't send her home.'

'Of course not.' Janet said.

They were low on staff numbers and would do their best to keep the observation ward closed for as long as possible.

At nine they hit the ground running.

Gladys would have to wait to be admitted. For now her gurney was parked in the corridor where the staff could keep an eye on her without her taking up a cubicle or having to open the observation ward.

She lay there, singing, and didn't seem to mind at all.

'It's supposed to be a Tuesday night!' Helene moaned as the place started to look more like

Accident and Emergency on a Saturday after the pubs had turned out than a weeknight.

A group of young men, all the worse for wear, were creating a bit of a ruckus in the waiting room. The security guards were in there, watching them, as Adele called one of the men through.

It wasn't even ten o'clock and the place was full.

She put on some gloves and peeled back the dressing that the triage nurse had put over his eye.

'Sorry, Oliver,' she said as he winced. 'That must hurt.'

It was a nasty cut and was going to require a lot of stitches.

Phillip came in and introduced himself and then took a careful look at the wound.

He was a nice doctor, calm and laid back, and Adele would always remember how kind he had been to her the day he had broken the awful news.

Phillip never referred to it and Adele was grateful for that.

Now, though, she understood the tears in his

eyes that day. Phillip was very much a family man and he had a daughter close in age to Adele.

'I want to take my time to suture this,' Phillip told Oliver. 'Which means you might have to wait for a few hours until I'm able to give it the attention it deserves.'

The patient nodded.

'For now, Adele will put on a saline dressing to keep it moist. Adele,' Phillip asked, 'is the overnight ward open?'

'It's about to be.' Adele nodded.

She was going to take Gladys around after this.

'Well, why don't we admit you there?' Phillip said to his patient. 'You can get some rest and then when the place is quiet I'll come and suture you.' He turned to Adele. 'Hourly obs, please.'

'Sure.'

Adele started to dress the laceration as Phillip wrote up his notes and then he opened up the curtain to head out to see the next patient.

It was then Adele heard an angry shout. 'There he is!'

It all happened very quickly after that.

A group of men—not the ones from the waiting room—had come into the corridor and had found who they were looking for.

They barged Phillip aside, and he was knocked to the floor and trampled over in their haste to get to Oliver.

Unfortunately for Adele, she was now the only thing between them and the man they wanted. As Oliver went to jump down, the gurney moved and the punch aimed at Oliver hit Adele's cheek. She fell to one side, her fall broken by a metal trolley to her middle.

It was over in seconds.

The security guards hauled the men out of the cubicle and Adele found out the police had already been alerted as soon as the group had burst into the department.

She could hear the sirens.

Janet moved her away from the drama and onto the computer chair at the nurses station and Adele just sat there, feeling her eye and trying to work out what had just happened.

'You'll be okay,' Janet said as she checked her eye.

And then Adele remembered Phillip and that he had been knocked to the floor.

'How's Phillip?' she asked.

'He's a bit winded. He's in his office. Helene's with him.'

No work was getting done.

The night manager was on her way down and would arrange cover. Ambulances would be placed on bypass for now as the department dealt with what was, unfortunately, not a particularly rare occurrence.

Helene came around then and brought Janet up to date. 'Phillip's okay,' she said. 'Just a few bruises and his glasses are broken.'

'Is Zahir on his way?' Janet checked.

'He's fifteen minutes away,' Helene replied.

Zahir would make it in ten.

CHAPTER SIX

ZAHIR WAS TAKING Bella home when the phone call came in.

Rather, he was taking Bella back to her apartment.

They had loosely dated for a few weeks and though he had been upfront from the start—that they would go nowhere—Bella seemed to have completely blanked out that particular conversation.

When she had rung to say she had tickets to the theatre, Zahir had told her that he was considering going home.

'I could come over and visit.'

For Zahir it was by far the worst suggestion she could have made.

But it wasn't the rules of his land that made him end things.

He just couldn't ignore his feelings for Adele any more and he was certain that they were reciprocated. Perhaps it wasn't such a foolish idea for her to see where he lived.

If he was going to fight for them.

Zahir had never run from a challenge, yet he knew this was perhaps an impossible one.

Now he chose to face it.

Zahir hadn't rushed from Emergency to take Bella out.

Instead, he had stopped by to visit his mother.

After that he had dropped in at Emergency to hopefully speak with Adele but she was busy making out with a mannequin and making others laugh.

And at the theatre, instead of watching the performance, he had sat in the dark, thinking about Adele and what she had been through.

Who was he to deny her a holiday?

He loved his homeland very much.

Oh, there were problems. Serious ones at that. Yet there was a certain magic to Mamlakat Almas that Adele deserved to experience.

He knew, even if she would be looking after his mother, that she would be beautifully taken care of at the palace. He thought of the golden desert and the lush oases. He thought of steam rising from hot springs and the majesty of the stars at night. How, no matter how many problems you had, the night sky held you in such awe that it reduced them. So much so that sometimes you simply forgot your troubles completely.

Adele could certainly use that.

And as for the two of them?

He didn't know the answer—just that they could not end without a chance.

He was just about to launch into his *it's not you, it's me* speech with Bella when his phone had rung.

Seeing that it was the hospital, he took the call, hoping that there wasn't a problem with his mother.

It was Helene and she sounded somewhat breathless.

'Zahir, there's been a gang fight in the emergency department and some of the staff were in the middle of it. A couple have been injured, not seriously, though.'

'Who?' Even as he asked the question he was executing a U-turn.

'Phillip. He's got a few bruises and his glasses are broken. Adele has a black eye and is a bit winded, and Tony, the security guard, was kicked.'

As they approached the hospital Zahir could see blue lights from several police cars and vans outside the ambulance bay.

'Wait here,' he said to Bella as he pulled into his reserved spot.

Bella though had no intention of waiting in the car, he soon realised, because as he arrived at the nurses' station he turned and saw that she had followed him in.

'It just came from nowhere,' Janet explained to Zahir as he looked around the chaotic department. 'We were already busy. I don't think they intended to hit out at the nursing staff or the doctor. I'm sorry we had to call you in.'

'You were right to call me in,' he said. Phillip

was in no way fit to see patients and, as well as that, the staff deserved to be treated at times like this by the most senior staff.

He could see that Adele was sitting in a chair with her arms folded over her stomach. Her eye and cheek were swollen and she looked angry.

'Where's Phillip?' Zahir asked.

'He's in his office. Tony's already in a cubicle.'

'I want Adele and Phillip both in gowns and in cubicles.'

Zahir would do everything to keep this completely professional. As Janet was taking Adele to get changed, Bella chose her moment to speak.

'How long do you think you'll be?' she asked, and Zahir turned impatiently.

'Why don't you get a taxi home? I might be a while.'

'I'm happy to wait in your office.'

Adele heard the brief exchange as she made her way to the cubicle.

Janet had been wrong, it would seem. Bella hadn't been *gone by morning* and never had

Adele felt more drab in her baggy scrubs and showing the beginnings of a lovely black eye.

She could hear the sounds of the police radios and tried not to think back to the last time she had been in a cubicle, waiting for a doctor to arrive.

As he waited for Phillip and Adele to get changed, the receptionist, as was protocol, brought up Adele's old Accident and Emergency notes. He flicked through them and tried to be objective. He read about an eighteen-year-old nursing student with minor injuries who had been the driver in a high-impact motor vehicle accident.

Phillip had wanted to admit her to the observation ward but the patient had refused and said she wanted to go and wait near Theatre.

There was a self-discharge form attached to the notes that Adele had signed.

Everything was there, even her muted reaction when Phillip had broken the news that her mother was critically ill, was noted.

It just didn't seem enough, Zahir thought.

Yes, the notes were detailed but there was a

brevity to them, to all patient notes here, that Zahir could not logically explain to his colleagues.

First he checked in on Phillip. He now had spare glasses on but there was a small cut over his eye and a nasty bruise on his back. He checked Phillip's abdomen. 'Any tenderness?' he asked.

'A bit,' Phillip admitted.

'I would like his urine checked for blood,' he said to Janet, and then spoke with Phillip. 'I would like you to stay in overnight.'

'It might be better,' Phillip agreed. 'Meredith will get a fright if I come home in the middle of the night.'

Tony, the security guard, was next and he wanted to get back to work but, having examined him, Zahir said that he should go home.

'Adele.' He came in to see her with Janet. 'I'm so sorry that this happened.'

She didn't respond.

'How are you feeling?'

'Fantastic!' Adele knew her sarcastic response was perhaps a bit harsh but what hurt more than the bruise was that, after a year of being ignored, now that she was a patient he was finally being nice to her.

He went through everything and asked if she'd been knocked out.

'No.'

He went through all the allergies and her medical history and Adele answered him in a monotone.

'Are you on any medication?'

'No,' Adele said. 'Just the Pill.'

She didn't add it was the pill of perpetual hope, hope that one day she would be doing what seemingly every other twenty-four-year-old had already done.

It really wasn't the best of nights.

He picked up the torch and checked her pupils' responses. He tried not to notice unshed tears, but he could see her pain. Oh, his findings were not evidence based, but he could see that there were years of agony there.

'I need to look at the back of your eye.'

He picked up ophthalmoscope and Adele stared

ahead as he moved in close. She managed not to blink and then thankfully it was over.

She felt as if he had just stared into the murky depths of her soul.

His fingers gently probed the swelling around her eye.

'It's a soft-tissue injury,' Zahir said.

'I know.'

'It needs to be iced but you are going to have a black eye. Is it painful?'

'No.'

It was the truth. It didn't really hurt, as such. What pained her more was the shock of what had happened and the indignity of Zahir now being kind to her.

'I need now to look at your stomach,' Zahir said.

'I was just winded.'

'Adele,' Zahir said, 'this will probably go to court and my notes need to be thorough. Lie down, please.'

She did so and Janet covered her neatly with the blanket before lifting her gown. He examined her abdomen and she answered the question before he asked it.

'There's no tenderness,' she said as he probed her stomach. And then she gave a wry laugh.

She hadn't just been talking about her abdomen—there had never been any tenderness from him.

'Did I miss the joke?' Zahir asked, and he gave her a smile as he covered her with the blanket.

And maybe because she was hurting so badly she was allowed to be a little bit mean too.

'I don't need your small talk and your pleasant bedside manner, Zahir,' she told him. 'We don't get on, let's just keep it that.'

She glanced to Janet, who gave her a small smile as if to say, *You get to say what you want to tonight.*

Janet had seen for herself the way that Zahir was with her, though she knew it had nothing to do with them not getting on!

'I would like you to stay in the observation ward tonight,' Zahir said.

'Well, I'd prefer to go home.'

'Who is there to look out for you?'

Adele thought of Helga and James and closed her eyes as Janet spoke. 'I'm not putting you in a taxi to go home to those flatmates tonight. I'm not going to be argued with on this, Adele.'

'Is Phillip going home?' Adele asked.

'Phillip is staying here tonight too,' Zahir answered the question. 'He doesn't want to upset his wife by turning up in the middle of the night.' His mind was made up. 'You're staying in and then I'll sign you off for the rest of the week.'

Adele would far rather have gone home but instead she had to lie there listening to Phillip snoring and Gladys, who was now in the opposite bed, first singing and later talking in her sleep.

And then she too started to snore!

As well as that there was a lot of chatter coming from the staffroom as people went for their breaks.

Yikes, she would be quieter in the future when she took her break, Adele decided.

A light was shining from the desk and Adele asked if the curtain could be pulled around her.

Then, just as she drifted off, it was time for her hourly observations.

And then, a while later, from the other side of the curtain came the balm of Zahir's voice as he asked the night nurse for an update.

'How's Gladys?'

'Sobering up.'

'How's Phillip?'

'His obs are all fine, he's sleeping soundly. What happened with Tony?'

'He was discharged home.'

And then he asked about her.

'What about Adele?'

'Her obs are stable, she's not sleeping very well, though.'

'Okay.'

Zahir went off to see some more patients.

It was an exceptionally busy night but in between seeing patients he made his *it's not you, it's me* speech to a very put-out Bella.

Normally he would have seen her home, but tonight he could not leave the department and he could not string her along so she had gone home in a taxi.

Now, as the day staff started to trickle in, Zahir made coffee.

And he took one in to Adele.

She was finally asleep, not that anyone took such a thing into consideration in the observation ward!

'Adele.'

He watched as she woke up and opened both eyes, and he was pleased to see that her eye had not closed over.

'How are you feeling?' he enquired.

'A bit sorry for myself,' she admitted. 'And I'm sorry if I was rude to you last night.'

'I get it.'

'I doubt it.' She sat up and saw that he was placing a mug of coffee on her locker.

'Ooh, I really am getting the royal treatment this morning,' she said, and then smiled at her own joke and Zahir found that he did too.

'I've discharged you,' he said. 'Roger comes on at seven and I shall bring him up to speed with all that happened last night and then I shall drive you home.'

'I don't want you to drive me home, Zahir,' she said.

She didn't.

All she needed was to get away from him, from the torture of being crazy about someone. He had been horrible to her, rude to her, and while she understood that he might not fancy her she loathed the sudden false niceness.

'I'm going to call a friend to come and get me,' Adele said.

'No, you're not,' Zahir refuted. 'We need to talk.'

'About?'

'We shall discuss things in the car.'

He made no secret that he was taking her home. In fact, when Phillip asked Adele how she was getting home, Zahir responded that he would take her himself.

And, really, no one gave it a thought.

Janet had offered her a lift and so had Helene and a couple of other staff too.

Of course her colleagues were concerned.

The mood was sombre and assaults on staff were not good for morale.

'Here.' Janet had fetched Adele's clothes from her locker and brought her a towel and the little overnight pack that Gladys and Phillip would be getting too.

It contained a tiny bar of soap, a minute tube of toothpaste, a toothbrush and a little plastic comb.

Adele freshened up and pulled on the tube skirt and top she had worn yesterday and slipped on shoes.

Zahir was waiting for her at the desk and speaking with Janet.

'I'm on my holidays!' Adele smiled. 'Do you think I'll pull?' And it made Janet laugh as she stood there with a huge black eye.

'Have a wonderful break, Adele,' Janet said, as Adele walked out in the clothes she had arrived in, trying not to be just a little more disillusioned with the world.

'Send us a postcard…'

They walked out and Adele winced at the bright morning sunlight.

'You're not very good at parking your car,' Adele commented, because it was over the line and at an angle.

He did not tell her the reason—that on hearing she had been injured he had hit the accelerator and when he had arrived he had practically run in to see how she was.

Instead, he held open the door for her.

Adele got in and a moment later he joined her.

'We meet again,' she said.

As he drove past the bus stop Zahir thought of all the times he had driven on, pretending not to have noticed her there.

And so did Adele.

She didn't understand why he briefly turned and smiled.

She didn't smile back.

'Are you sulking?' he asked.

'Yes, I'm sulking.'

'Are you warm enough?' he asked, because he had the air conditioner on up high.

'You can stop being nice now,' she said. 'I'm not your patient any more.'

'No, you're not. Adele, I have spoken with my mother. If you are still interested, she would love you to be her private nurse.'

'I don't need you feeling sorry for me, Zahir.'

'I spoke to her last night, before the incident.'

He had.

Zahir had thought long and hard about it.

He had been avoiding Adele for twelve months now and it had got him precisely nowhere.

He wasn't used to avoiding anything, yet his feelings for Adele could challenge a lifetime of thinking and centuries of tradition.

Wasn't he asking his father to do the same?

It was time to face things.

'On Monday she will fly home to Mamlakat Almas. A car would collect you at six in the morning and you would meet her at the airport… and you would return to England on a commercial flight two weeks later.'

Adele frowned.

'You don't have to worry about a uniform or what to wear, everything will be provided.'

She turned and looked at him and for the first time since last night she properly smiled. 'What does that even mean?'

'Just bring what you feel you want to. We are very used to having guests in the palace and accommodating them.'

'Oh.'

'And if you are worried about something, there will be someone who can advise you. It really will be relaxing and you need that. Especially after last night.'

Excitement started to ooze in, like jam squeezing out a sandwich as you took a bite, but Adele did what she could to rein it in for now as the car pulled up at her flat.

'I will do some studying up on hysterectomies...'

'Adele.' Zahir smiled. And in her direction too! 'It's a holiday. My mother will just need a little encouragement to walk, especially on the plane, and some reassurance, but we both know a private nurse is a touch unnecessary. She is, though, a queen. The second week would be yours to completely enjoy.'

'I want to see the desert,' Adele admitted.

'I'm sure it will be arranged.'

There was such energy between them, he knew that she felt it and how confused she must be by his cool treatment of her.

'You should go in,' he said, as still they sat outside her flat. 'Get some rest. You didn't sleep much last night.'

'I had Gladys singing and Phillip snoring.'

He said nothing, he was too deep in thought.

It was Adele who broke the silence.

'Thank you, Zahir. I know you didn't want me there but I really will take care of her.'

'I know you will. You will love my country. It really is magical.'

'I don't believe in magic,' Adele said. She had stopped believing in magic and miracles a very long time ago.

She had prayed so hard for her mother's recovery, and had later downgraded that plea to just the tiniest sign that her mother knew she was near.

Zahir looked at her bruise. 'You need to ice your eye.'

'I will.'

'And use some arnica cream.'

'Okay.'

For a second there she felt as if he was going to examine it again but though he raised his hand, he changed his mind.

And then, in that moment, she felt his resistance.

He hadn't been about to examine her.

Experience counted for nothing in this equation, for Adele had none, but she was quite sure then that she had been about to be kissed.

Maybe it was the knock to her head that was causing irrational thoughts.

Lack of sleep.

Too much want.

She needed to go, she knew, because she wanted to reach over and kiss him, and if she was reading things wrong she would never get over the shame.

She opened the car door and then, as she started to get out, she realised that she still had her seat belt on.

There could be no dignified exit, though, when there was a pulse beating between your legs.

She went to undo her belt.

He went to do the same.

For a year he had relied on self-control.

It was dissolving.

Zahir looked into the blue eyes he had wanted to explore since the very first day he had seen her.

She just stared back at him.

And then she remembered Bella, all beautiful and no doubt waiting in his home.

'How was the theatre?' she asked in a voice that was oddly high.

'Terrible,' Zahir said, though he knew what she meant. 'Bella and I broke up last night.'

'Because?' Adele asked.

'Because of this.'

Do what is essential, he had heard in the desert.

He had interpreted that as avoiding her, that it was essential to resist her. Now, though, it was essential that they kiss.

For Adele, after such a horrible night, came the sweetest, most unexpected reward.

The feel of his lips on hers.

He kissed her softly and was careful of her sore face.

And as she moaned to the bliss, he slipped in his tongue and she tasted perfection. She discovered all that had been missing and why a kiss had never worked till now.

It had needed to be his.

There was silence in her mind and the sensual soothing of his tongue. Her hand went to the back of his head, and she felt that silk hair on her fingers.

There was utter relief as he kissed her, soon replaced by the yearning for more.

He kissed her deeper and his hand slid from her waist to the stomach he had touched last night.

And now there *was* tenderness as his hand

slipped into her T-shirt and her skin was traced by him.

She knew then the hell he had gone through.

Trying to be friendly and to treat her as a patient.

And she knew now the reason for his seeming disdain.

His hand came up to her small breast and he stroked it through her bra and all this within a kiss.

'Does that explain things better?' he asked, as he moved his mouth a fraction away.

It did.

'Do you understand now why I didn't stop the car the other night?'

His hand was still on her breast and the ache between them could not be soothed by his soft caress.

'You should have,' she said.

'I would not have been tender then.'

'That would have been fine,' she said, and now she got the reward of his smile.

And always he was honest and upfront and explained to women that it could never come to anything.

It would possibly be fairer to say that now.

Yet he could not.

He removed his hand from her breast but hers was still on the back of his head and possibly it would require surgery to remove it, for she wanted to feel his lips again.

'Adele, this would be very much frowned upon back home.'

'I'm not going to tell your mum,' she teased, but now Zahir did not smile.

'I am returning home with the Queen.'

She swallowed and now she removed her hand and sat there and stared out of the window rather than at him. 'Because you don't trust me?'

'No,' Zahir said. 'I was always going to return with her. Do you see why I didn't want you there?'

She did.

'Why did you change your mind?' she asked.

'Because otherwise it would have been good-bye.'

She didn't understand.

'Go in,' he said.

'I don't want to.'

'Go in,' he said again. 'I will see you on Monday.'

'And?'

He didn't know.

All Zahir knew was...they had been awoken.

CHAPTER SEVEN

'READY FOR THE OFF?' Annie, her favourite nurse at the care home, asked on the night before Adele flew to Mamlakat Almas.

'I am!'

'You're eye's looking a lot better.'

Adele had been icing it regularly and using the arnica cream that Zahir had suggested. The spectacular purple bruise had now faded to pale yellow.

Sometimes she felt as if she had dreamt their kiss.

As if her mind, tired of nothing happening, had manufactured it.

Yet she knew it had been real and though the last few days had been busy she had dwelt on it regularly.

Hourly.

Maybe every five minutes or so!

Even though Zahir had said everything would be provided, she had spent a small fortune on underwear, nightdresses, dressing gowns and slippers in case she had to go the Queen at night.

It was very hard dressing for mother *and* son, Adele had thought as she'd closed her case on her hopefully subtly sexy lingerie.

But then she also knew there would be no furtive kisses or hot sensual Arabian nights.

She would be working and Zahir had told her anything more would be very much frowned on at his home.

And, from the little she knew, things were different there and her lovely new underwear had no hope of being seen.

Still, it was better to be safe than sorry!

'It will just be for two weeks,' she told her mum as she kissed her goodbye.

Yet it was about more than a two-week break. Adele knew that by taking this step she was if not cutting the cord then loosening it a touch.

Annie did too.

'You know we'll take good care of her.'

'I know that you will and I'll call every day.'

As she left the nursing home Adele felt different.

Of course she would be back and she would always visit but this was a huge step in reclaiming her life.

It was very hard to get to sleep and it felt that as soon as she did her alarm went off.

The car duly arrived and Adele was only too happy to close the door on the flatmates from hell.

She had bought some linen trousers and a long-sleeved top for the journey and then regretted it as her trousers had already crumpled while waiting for the car to arrive.

The driver made small talk as he drove her to Heathrow, but they took a different entrance from the main one. Soon she was in a very plush room and there was Leila but there was no sign of Zahir.

Leila had the pale, sickly pallor of someone who had spent time in hospital and indoors but apart from that she seemed well. 'I am so pleased to see you, Adele.' She beamed. 'This is Hannah, one of the nurses who has been taking care of me at the hotel.'

There was a detailed handover.

Leila had seen Mr Oman for a post-operative check-up the day before and Adele was told that he was very pleased with her progress.

'This is his phone number,' Hannah said, as she went through the file. 'You are to ring him if there are any concerns. Here is a course of antibiotics for Queen Leila, if he feels it necessary for her to take them. However, Mr Oman also said that he has full faith that the healers can care for her from this point on. He has written a letter for them. They can also contact him with any concerns that they might have.'

Hannah said goodbye and Adele looked out at the royal jet, scarcely able to believe that soon they would be boarding.

'I am so excited to be going home,' Leila said. 'Zahir and Dakan should be here soon.'

And here they were.

Always, *always*, he looked immaculate.

Just not today.

His suit looked a bit rumpled, as if he had slept in it, and he really needed to shave.

Oh, she hoped he didn't!

Adele hadn't seen or heard from Zahir since they had kissed, and she tried to remember how she used to greet him before...

That's right, she'd smile and he'd ignore her!

It had worked for twelve months and it worked now, for Adele smiled and Zahir duly ignored her.

It was Dakan who returned her smile.

In fact, he came over. 'My mother's ever so pleased that you're going home with her. I brought some antibiotics just in case they were required...'

'It's okay,' Adele said. 'Mr Oman has already taken care of that.'

'These are for you,' Dakan said, 'in case you need them. Are you allergic to anything?'

'No but—'

'Adele, believe me, you don't want to get ill there. I'm sure Zahir has got some with him but he may well be busy or away. Have these with you just in case.'

'Thank you.'

A flight steward came out to greet Leila and Dakan went over to his mother and they embraced.

Leila's eyes filled with tears and, though they spoke in Arabic, it was clear to Adele that Leila found it hard to say goodbye and that she wanted both of her sons home.

It was time to board and Leila did so without fuss, though she needed a little help with the steep stairs.

Adele felt dizzy with anticipation as she boarded the royal jet and Leila greeted the captain, co-pilot and the rest of the crew.

They greeted her so formally—even Hannah had called her Queen Leila—that Adele realised the great privilege it had been to talk to Leila so informally.

The Queen and Zahir sat in a lounge area and Adele did what she could to make Leila comfortable. She gave her a little cushion to put over her incision and helped her to strap in for take-off.

'Are you wearing your anti-embolism stockings?'

'I am.' Leila nodded, and lifted the bottom of her robe to show that she was.

'Good,' Adele said.

Adele was guided a little further back to a gorgeous leather seat that was set apart from the lounge, but she would be able to watch the Queen and would hear her if she called. She was told that her room was further down at the rear of the plane and she could sleep there later.

Adele had thought maybe it would be small jet, but it was huge, and lavishly furnished.

Still, she tried to focus on Leila.

It was the most rapid take off. Almost as soon as Adele sat down the plane started moving and before long they were levelling out. Adele looked down and saw they were already over water and when she noticed Zahir looking at her she gave him a small smile.

This was normal to him.

It was a huge adventure to her.

Once they were able to move around Adele found her room. It was small but there was a very comfortable-looking bed and a small shower. It was like first-class travel and this was just for the staff! There was a muslin nightdress laid out for her on the bed.

As well as that, hanging up was a coral-coloured robe and some pretty jewelled shoes.

She thought about what Zahir had said about everything being provided and it felt as if she had entered another world.

She came out and Zahir was on his computer and was chatting with his mother when the meals were served.

Adele took her cues from the flight stewards. She was seated to the rear and would take her meal there, whereas Zahir and Leila ate at a polished table.

Adele chose a lovely mint soup and a small bread roll for starters but her stomach was too tied in knots to have a main course.

Dessert was a light, pale custard with a rich rose-water syrup over it.

She saw that Zahir had declined dessert.

A foolish mistake, Adele thought, and closed her eyes in bliss at the taste and then opened them to see him.

He made her blush.

With one glance from Zahir she felt heat in her face.

Once the meals had been cleared away, Zahir declared he was going to bed.

He went into his suite, stripped off and showered.

He hadn't slept last night. He had gone out but had soon returned to his apartment and drunk cognac, wondering when, if and under what circumstances he might return to England.

He pulled on black silk lounge pants and closed his eyes but sleep would not come.

Zahir, in an attempt to drag his mind from Adele and those awful linen trousers, made a couple of phone calls to some architects and tried to line up some meetings.

One of them, Nira, sounded promising and she had some questions that she put to him.

Adele, on the other hand, tried not to think of Zahir asleep a matter of metres away as Leila took out her sewing.

'Come and see this, Adele,' Leila said.

'Oh!' Adele walked over and looked down, and saw that the Queen was embroidering a small square. The silks were so rich and the stitching so detailed it really was exquisite. 'It's beautiful. What are you making?'

'A blanket,' Leila told her. 'I have been making it for many, many years.' She took out a few squares from the sewing bag for Adele to see. They were all different, and each one was a work of art in itself. They ranged from flowers, to delicate letters, to beautiful coloured birds.

'These must take hours and hours.'

'They do,' Leila agreed. 'It is a stitching technique that has been passed on through generations. Each square has a different symbol or flower…soon I shall put them all together. It has been a labour of love.'

Soon, though, Leila put away her embroidery and declared that she was very tired. 'I don't understand why, though, I slept well last night.'

'You were up early,' Adele pointed out.

'I am always up early.'

'It's your first proper outing since surgery, so being tired is to be expected,' Adele said.

'Well, I'm going to go to bed, if you could come and help me.'

'Of course, but you do need to walk around first.'

The Queen wasn't sitting in cramped economy class but she had just undergone abdominal surgery and that was a major risk factor for embolisms.

'You're bossy,' Leila moaned, and then she smiled at Zahir, who had come out of his room and was on his phone.

Of course, Leila didn't nearly faint at the sight of Zahir in black silk lounge pants and a naked torso.

That would be Adele.

And neither did Leila care that his hair was wet from the shower and that his feet were bare.

That would be Adele too.

Oh, she tried not to notice him speaking in Arabic into his phone as he opened up the laptop he had left in the lounge.

Finally Adele walked Leila to her room and it was Adele rather than Leila who breathed out a sigh of relief as she closed the door on Zahir.

It was as beautiful as any five-star hotel.

There was a large walnut dressing table and a pretty lemon-coloured bed, which had been turned back.

Adele helped Leila to change into a nightgown and then Leila sat on the edge of the bed and Adele helped her with her legs.

Really, she was unsure whether Leila could not manage or simply was not used to doing it herself.

'I'll come and wake you in a couple of hours so that you can do some leg exercises.'

'Very well. If I need you or I am concerned

about something I shall have a stewardess alert you, but now it is time for you to get some rest too, Adele,' Leila said. She could be bossy too! 'There should be a robe for you to change into before we land. There will be more of a selection for you when we get to Mamlakat Almas. Could you please dim my light on your way out?'

Adele did so.

'Thank you,' Leila said. 'Now you go and relax.'

It was incredibly hard to, though, especially when she came out of the Queen's bedroom and saw that Zahir was still talking on the phone.

She went to sit on her allocated seat and then changed her mind and decided to head to her own room, but Zahir ended the call then.

'Adele, come and sit in the lounge.'

'No.' Adele shook her head. She was blushing, but not from embarrassment. She was heated and turned on just at the sight of him and the memory of their kiss. Sitting on a sofa with him dressed in next to nothing had no chance of ending well.

He knew what was on her mind.

'No staff will come unless they are summoned.'

'What if your mother gets up?'

He smiled.

'My mother doesn't get out of bed without the help of a maid. You'll know when she wants to get up! Come on.' He gestured with his head for her to join him. 'We need to talk.'

They did and so Adele went over.

She went to sit on a chair but he patted the seat on the sofa beside him and rather tentatively she sat down.

'I was just speaking with an architect and arranging to meet.' He pointed to his laptop screen and she saw building plans.

'I'm not returning to London, I haven't renewed my contract,' Zahir, rather bluntly, told her. 'I am hoping to bring about change to the health system…' He gave a small mirthless laugh. 'Actually, there *is* no real system.'

'None?'

'There is one small hospital but it is under-resourced and overstretched. Most doctors stay a month and leave and I don't blame them. My father is resistant to change.'

'When you say you're not coming back, for how long?'

'Maybe never.' And he was brutally honest then. 'I have long held off on marriage, but my father will insist on it if change gets under way.'

And just as that evening when she had seen the flowers, and had known they had not come from him, today she knew that marriage could not apply to her.

'There are many traditions and legends and rules in my land,' Zahir explained. 'I could take the whole flight to tell you about them and only then would we scratch the surface. The main thing I am trying to explain is that I cannot see my country accepting you. That is why I have done nothing about us.'

'Zahir, I don't want to live there,' Adele said. 'I would never leave my mother for a start, but we could have had a year, Zahir. A whole year of...'

And she felt like slapping his cheek for his restraint. 'Now you're leaving, just as I find out you wanted me all along. Why did you tell me all this now when there's nothing we can do? Why did you say to your mother I could come when you knew you were going to marry? Why kiss me…?'

'Would you prefer that I hadn't?' he asked. 'I could have left, and let you carry on assuming that I disliked you. You could have had your holiday in France and returned and found out I had gone…'

She tried to picture it and she didn't like what she saw.

'Perhaps I would have returned in a few years' time and by then I'd be married, perhaps you would be too.'

And she sat there.

'All I can tell you is that I was not ready to say goodbye and had you not come today, it would have been goodbye, Adele.'

'What happens now?'

He shrugged his broad shoulders.

'That's no answer.'

'Because I haven't been to the desert to ask for a solution.'

No, she did not understand their ways.

Neither, fully, did he.

He had sought solutions under the sun and the stars on many occasions.

The answers were always the same but in various orders.

Do what is essential.

Be patient.

In time the answers will unfold.

Yet they hadn't.

He did not want his father to die, yet that was the only solution that Zahir could see.

'Adele, it was either say goodbye in the car that morning and you would never know how I feel, or bring you to my home. I chose the latter.'

Adele looked into his beautiful eyes and she was now very glad that he had.

To have never known his kiss, to have never sat here looking him in the eye, as painful as it might prove, she was glad to be here.

There was an ache for contact and he solved that with his thumb, running it along her bottom lip.

'I want to kiss you,' he said, and he looked at her mouth as he spoke.

'Someone might come.'

'Not unless I summon them.'

And she looked at his mouth too.

'Leila might call. Anyway, I'm working.'

'If you are needed they will buzz through to your room.'

She half expected the oxygen masks to suddenly ping down, she felt so light-headed.

'This might be the last chance,' Zahir said, and he saw the struggle in her eyes.

'Just a kiss?' Adele checked, because just a kiss surely couldn't be wrong.

'Just that,' he said.

She stood on legs that felt unfamiliar and walked the length of the lounge and past the Queen's room.

There were no staff around, the only sounds the engines and her own pulse whooshing in her ears.

She stepped into the small bedroom and told herself that there was no chance they would be caught.

Yet she knew this was wrong.

Zahir came in then and turned the lock on the door.

All this for a kiss.

'One kiss,' Adele said, as he went for the drawstring of her linen pants.

'Just one,' Zahir said, and her thighs were shaking as she stepped out of her clothes.

She lifted her arms and he peeled off her top.

He unhooked her new and very lacy bra and peeled it down her arms and his eyes took in her small breasts and looked down at her stomach.

Her knickers were silver and tiny and he could see the dark blond hair peeking out the top.

And Adele could see him hard beneath black silk.

She looked at his solid chest and broad shoulders. With this kiss their skin would make first contact. She lowered her head to taste his broad muscled chest.

'Don't waste your one kiss there,' he said.

His voice was gravelly and thick with desire and Adele felt as if hands had closed around her throat because she was struggling to breathe.

He moved her so that her back was to the wall

and as she went to reach for him he took her wrists and raised them so that they were above her head and then he held them against the wall. He looked at the lift of her breasts and how she was shaking with arousal.

'You're presumptuous,' Adele accused, and he smiled a slow smile.

'I am.'

He restrained her yet his own restraint was gone and he kissed her so hard that their teeth clashed.

One kiss, which made Adele twist against the restraint of his hands as she fought for her chance to hold him and drag him in.

He denied it.

One kiss, where their chests finally met, and she wanted to move her mouth just to taste his shoulder but that would break the deal of one kiss.

Her breasts flattened against him as he crushed her.

His erection slid against her stomach and she wanted it lower. He just bored into her and, with a craving for more contact, with nothing else for it, she attempted to hook her leg around him, but he widened his stance so that her foot dropped to the floor.

But now he was lower.

His tongue moved with the same motion as his groin and it was still one kiss but it had been spiced with dynamite.

Her jaw ached with tension and that tension slid to her neck and raced down her spine. Her thighs pressed together and Adele was rocking her groin into him. As she started to shudder he released her hands.

She held him between them as she came, and he felt the rip of tension and the stilling of her tongue, the slight squeal that he swallowed as she gripped him hard.

And it was still just one kiss as he silvered her palm and fingers and Adele felt him hot on her stomach as they pressed into each other.

Then he kissed her back but not to reality, for that was lost to her now.

And then he was gone.

CHAPTER EIGHT

ADELE SHOWERED AND put on the little muslin robe and, quite simply, she crashed.

She fell into a deep, dreamless sleep and yet woke with instant and absolute recall and with a curious absence of guilt.

She just lay listening to the hum of the plane and tried to understand how she was feeling.

It was disorientating.

Not just that she was on the way to a strange land but the might of his want and the rage of her desire.

There was no compass, no goalpost, no promises made, other than that he would ask the desert for solution.

Adele got out of bed and looked out of the window and there below her were the golden orange sands that Zahir would be communing with soon.

'I'd like the solution too,' she said, not quite tongue in cheek, because it was so vast and so endless that she first glimpsed its power.

She dressed in the pretty coral robe and put on her jewelled slippers and then looked at her reflection in the mirror on the door.

Adele barely recognised herself—not just her clothes, she should surely be on her knees in guilt and shame.

Yet she smiled.

Her intercom buzzed and she was informed that the Queen was awake and would like some assistance.

Adele knocked and went in and then blinked in surprise when she saw that Leila was in the bathroom, relaxing in a deep bath with taps made of gold.

There were bubbles up to her neck and she smiled as Adele came in.

'I didn't know you could have baths on a plane,' Adele admitted.

'You can have anything,' Leila said. 'The maid ran it for me, though I do need your help to get out.'

Adele helped her to step out and once Leila was dry Adele checked her wounds. There were three small ones from the laparoscopic procedure and all looked dry and healthy.

'I still have trouble with the stairs,' Leila admitted.

'It's quite a big operation,' Adele said. 'I think you're doing very well.'

'I am a bit nervous to go home,' Leila admitted as Adele helped her to dress. 'My husband has been so concerned. We've never been apart for so long and of course he is cross that I never told him I was having surgery. My husband is such a...' She stopped herself from saying anything more.

'You can talk to me,' Adele said. 'I would never break your confidence.'

'Even with Zahir?'

'Especially with Zahir,' Adele said. 'You're my patient and he's not your doctor, he's your son.

If I have any concerns I would speak with Mr Oman.'

'My husband is very stubborn and Zahir wants to make changes,' Leila said. 'Maybe I am worrying over nothing. I am a bit weepy. It says in the leaflet to expect to be.'

She handed the leaflet to Adele and she read it as the Queen spoke.

'I don't have to worry about not doing housework or heavy lifting,' Leila said.

'And no intercourse for six weeks,' Adele added.

She would not avoid subjects just because Leila was a queen.

'Poor Fatiq.' Leila smiled and then she surprised Adele. 'Poor me. I do think six weeks is a bit excessive.'

Adele remembered her time in training and often the women would joke that they'd consider it a little holiday, or ask if the doctor could change it to ten weeks instead.

No wonder the Al Rahal brothers came with

reputations. It would seem that the whole family was highly sexed.

'I hate sleeping alone.' Leila pouted.

'You can still share a bed.' Adele smiled but Leila shook her head.

'We have to sleep separately till I am healed. It was the same when I had my babies.'

Oh, no, Adele thought. At the time they must have needed each other most they had been apart.

'Once I am home I shall meet with the healer,' Leila told Adele. 'I'm sure I will feel brighter then.'

The Queen had selected a gown in a very deep shade of fuchsia and for someone who had just had surgery she looked stunning.

'I am going to do my make-up,' Leila told Adele, 'and then I'll be out.'

Adele sat in her seat and breakfast was served. She watched as Leila came out and took a seat at the gleaming table and then she turned her head and smiled.

And Adele fought not to.

It was Zahir.

As he walked past she quickly averted her eyes and looked out at the ocean.

He was wearing black robes and a *keffiyeh* that was tied with a rope of silver.

She looked again and saw that his feet were strapped in leather and that he was holding a scabbard that contained a long sword, which he put down on the sofa with the same ease Adele might put down her bag.

She had only ever seen him in a suit or scrubs, sometimes in jeans if he came in at night...

Adele had known the day they had met that he was a crown prince, but she had never really given it proper thought.

He had always been Zahir, Emergency Consultant, and the man she'd had a serious crush on.

Not any more.

Before her eyes he had become Crown Prince Sheikh Zahir Al Rahal, of Mamlakat Almas.

And that was scary at best.

Breakfast was cleared and they all took their seats.

Now the jet descended and to the right she

could see a glittering ocean and then a palace. As beautiful as it was, Adele knew that soon, if they were discovered, she might not be welcome here.

As they landed she watched as he picked up the leather scabbard from the sofa and put it on.

The hilt of his sword was jewelled and for a brief second he looked up and their eyes met.

She was used to him flicking his gaze away.

Now she knew why.

Adele stood by Leila's side to help her down the steps as the cockpit door opened.

The Queen had wrapped a scarf around her head and over her mouth and Adele attempted to do the same with hers.

The wind gave her the first taste of the desert.

Her scarf slid straight down and the hot air burnt in her lungs and she thought of the traditions and legends that Zahir had touched upon.

She doubted the desert was welcoming her.

CHAPTER NINE

THEY WERE DRIVEN the short distance from the runway to the palace.

As the car slowed to a halt Adele was pleasantly surprised when the door opened and she realised that it was Fatiq who had rushed to help his wife out of the car.

Leila gave a small cry of delight when she saw him and he was clearly pleased to see his wife and greeted her warmly.

For a moment Adele relaxed and she almost forgot he was a king.

But then she saw the look he shot at Zahir and she would never forget again.

They came into the entrance and Leila smiled at Adele. 'I am going to go up to my suite. You will be taken care of.'

'Thank you. Would you like me to help you up the stairs?' Adele offered.

'I will be fine.'

As Fatiq helped Leila up the steps she paused and held onto her stomach midway and bent over a little and he looked down at Zahir again.

Zahir stared back and Adele could feel the stand-off between the two men and it gave her goosebumps.

'Samina will take care of you from now,' Zahir informed her, and he walked off. She watched as guards opened two large engraved doors, which he went through.

The palace was splendid, and Adele had only seen the entrance.

There was a gentle, cool breeze and tiny hummingbirds were taking nectar from flowers even though they were inside. She looked at the dark staircase and ancient walls and heard the delicate sound of fountains.

She was shown to her suite and, as Leila had said, there was a stunning array of gowns for her to choose from.

Samina gave her some lessons, such as how to tie a scarf so it did not slide down and how to greet the King or Queen if they passed in the corridor.

'We have a system,' Samina explained. 'If Queen Leila needs you, she will summon you with this...' There was a small tablet by the bed. 'If you are not in your suite the message will go directly to your phone.'

It was a surprisingly modern system, yet there was nothing modern about her suite which was beautiful.

There was a velvet rope above her bed, which Adele was told she was to use to summon meals. There was a carved stone stairway that led down to her own beach and, as she walked through the large lounge, Samina opened some shutters and Adele looked down at a stunning mosaic pool below that was hers to enjoy.

'It is very private,' Samina explained. 'You can swim and if you want refreshments brought out to you, just pull the bell on the wall there.' She pointed down to it. 'Would you like supper here in your suite or down by the pool?'

Adele chose the pool.

It was so tranquil.

Even here tiny hummingbirds hovered and sipped nectar from the flowers, yet despite the gorgeous surroundings Leila couldn't quite relax.

She had seen the look Fatiq had given his son. He blamed Zahir for his wife having surgery.

Adele was starting to understand just how resistant the King was to change.

And that left her and Zahir nowhere.

She called the nursing home and was told that her mother appeared comfortable and that there was no change.

There never was.

Later, Leila paged her and said that the palace healer would like to meet with her.

Samina took Adele through to the King and Queen's wing and showed her to Leila's room.

Outside was a robed man, who followed Leila inside.

He was introduced to her as the palace healer.

Adele gave him the letter that Mr Oman had written and he read it and then spoke a little with Leila.

After he had gone she and Leila enjoyed a gentle stroll around the gardens. The sun was starting to set and there was the lovely sweet fragrance of jasmine.

'Is it good to be home?' Adele asked.

'So good,' Leila said. 'I will enjoy the peace for now. Things are going to get very busy soon now that Zahir is back. My husband wants to move ahead with a selection ceremony so that Zahir can choose his bride, but I have said I am too weak for that just now. In a month's time perhaps.'

And, yes, as much as it had hurt to hear it from Zahir, she was glad he had warned her so that she did not hear it first from his mother.

In the first few days, while Adele had worried she might be unnecessary, blissful as it was to mainly relax, she realised that Leila had been right to request a nurse to care for her in her home.

The Queen had some minor post-operative problems, which Adele was pleased to reassure her often happened.

'I shall call Mr Oman and see if you need antibiotics.'

'I want to speak with the palace healer also.'

Leila had seen him on the day she had arrived home but it had been a brief visit.

This was a more comprehensive consultation. He came to the Queen's chambers and they spoke at length. Leila translated what was said.

'He suggests that, starting tomorrow, I walk barefoot on the sand and that shall help my genitals and get me grounded.'

Adele blinked.

'He wants me to take a course in the healing baths. I have to have another woman come with me. That will be you. He is also going to speak with the *attar* and have him prepare a remedy.' Leila spoke with him again but they both were looking at Adele. 'He says you carry too much tension in your solar plexus.' Leila gave her a smile. 'I agree.'

Adele nodded yet she was troubled, especially when a maid came to her room the following morning with a muslin bathing dress that she was to wear under her robe and also a slender vial from the *attar*.

'This is for the Queen?' Adele checked, deciding that she would call Mr Oman before she administered it.

'No,' the maid said. 'The Queen already has her remedy. This has been prepared for you. You are to keep it at body temperature and carry it in your robe, and take a sip morning and night.'

'For me? But what's in it?'

The maid didn't answer and, troubled about what the Queen had been given, Adele decided to call Mr Oman. She was surprised to find he had already had a long conversation with the healer.

'Yes, he discussed it with me,' Mr Oman said. 'I agree that Leila should be out in the sun and the herbs he recommends are an excellent choice. Make sure she completes the antibiotics.'

They had a gorgeous morning, walking barefoot on the beach, and then Adele helped Leila down some stones steps. The healing baths were cut into rocks and filled by the ocean, and they took off their robes and got in.

It was bliss.

Unlike the ocean, here the water was calm and there was just the occasional gentle lulling wave.

'I needed this.' Leila closed her eyes and lay on her back and Adele found she was soon doing the same. 'The nurse at the hospital put salt in my bath, but of course it cannot match the magic of the ocean.'

Colour was returning to Leila's face and as the days passed, Adele realised just how tense she herself had been because she was starting to unwind.

Maybe she should try the remedy.

Adele didn't know why, all she knew was that she felt relaxed here.

That afternoon, when Leila had gone for a rest, instead of walking towards the beach, as she did most afternoons, Adele headed to the desert-facing side of the palace.

And it was there, for the first time since arriving, that she saw him.

Zahir was driving out through his own private exit when he saw Adele.

Her hair was blonder from swimming in the ocean and her cheeks were pinker. She looked very beautiful in a lilac robe and silver scarf.

He slowed the car to a stop and got out and she walked towards him.

'Am I not supposed to be here?' Adele checked.

'You can walk anywhere,' he said, 'unless it is gated. Don't worry, you cannot accidentally access the royal beach or gardens, they are all guarded. Just wander as you please.'

'I shall, then.'

He looked amazing in his robes and the *keffiyeh* brought out the silver in his eyes. He no longer had stubble on his jaw, it was way more than that, and he was simply beautiful.

'How has your time here been?' he asked her.

'Amazing,' Adele said. 'I can't say I've really been working...'

'My mother is very pleased that you are here. She said you have been liaising with Mr Oman.'

Adele nodded.

'And she says that the healer prescribed you a remedy.'

'He did,' Adele said. 'I don't know whether I should take it. I don't know what's in it.'

Zahir smiled and when he did, her stomach turned into a gymnast, because it didn't just somersault, it felt as it was tumbling over and over.

'Do you have it with you?' he asked, for he knew how things worked and that a potion should be carried by the recipient and kept at body temperature.

She nodded and went into her robe and handed over the vial.

He read the intricate writing that she could not understand.

'It's fine to drink, though just a sip morning and night,' Zahir told her. 'Do you know, my father and I were just talking and he pointed out that both Dakan and I have never been ill? He is right. I remember when I was studying medicine and I joined the rugby team. I strained my shoulder. I was new in London and I was surprised that they strapped it and suggested pain and anti-inflammatory medication. I ended up at a Chinese herbalist.'

'Did it help?'

'Yes,' Zahir said. 'It did.'

He had returned to Mamlakat Almas so gung-ho and demanding yet he could see the rapid improvement in his mother and he was quietly pleased that the healer had taken some time for Adele also.

She carried pain.

Emotional pain.

It was something he could both see and feel and something modern medicine had little room for.

He had seen it when he had shone the torch into her eyes, but he had expected to see it then. She had been hit after all. But the pain he had seen wasn't acute.

It was chronic.

Layer upon layer of pain.

He could only imagine his colleagues' reactions if he had written that in his notes.

'I am just going to look at the site for the new hospital.'

'Are the plans going well?'

'No,' Zahir admitted. 'Would you like to join me?'

'Is it allowed?'

'Of course,' he said. 'If the hospital goes ahead we would need nurses. Why wouldn't I seek your opinion?'

He was giving her the same explanation he would give his father. The truth was, he wanted some time with her.

It had been a long week, knowing that she was here and wondering how she was doing but being unable to enquire.

It was lovely to be out with Zahir.

He drove the car through ancient, dusty streets and then through a very modern city, at least in part.

There was an eclectic mix of ancient and modern. The most fashionable boutiques were housed in ancient buildings and there were locals and tourists, bikes and old cars along with sports cars and stretch limousines. Then there were towering modern hotels.

'We have everything but a workable health system,' Zahir told her. 'We have a good education system yet our best brains travel overseas to study medicine and few want to work back here once they have.'

They drove a little further and came to a small, rundown-looking building.

'This is the medical centre,' he explained.

They walked in and he spoke with a nervous receptionist who quickly summoned someone, a young woman, who showed them through the facility.

There was some very basic equipment and an occasional gleaming piece of machinery.

'Dakan and I bought these defibrillators last year. The trouble is, we need to train people in their use. It is a multi-faceted problem. This is the theatre...'

They stepped in and Adele could see why the Queen would seek treatment elsewhere.

'What do you see happening?' Adele asked. 'Tear it down and start again?'

'No.' He shook his head. 'This building should be the gateway to the new, though that is not my idea…' He led her through and they walked outside. The heat hit them like an open oven door and, in contrast to the busy street at the front, to the rear there was a vast expanse of nothing and they looked out to the desert.

'Like most cities, it is overcrowded and there is a clamour for space, yet this land had been held back for generations. The architects and advisors of the time knew that the city would one day need more room. I cannot build anything, though, without the King's approval. I want a facility that incorporates both traditional and modern medicine. I want them combined.'

'It would be amazing,' Adele said. 'What about the healers? Would they agree?'

'We are all healers,' Zahir said. 'It is time to put ego aside and to exchange knowledge and respect each other's ways. It was the palace healer who suggested my mother seek treatment elsewhere.'

They walked through the building and out to the car.

'I should get you back,' Zahir said.

He made absolutely no reference to the two of them and she looked out of the car window at a large sun in a pink sky. 'I'd love to see the desert.'

'I will see that it is arranged,' Zahir said.

They both knew that it wasn't what she had meant.

She'd wanted to know if he had sought solutions about them, but more than that she wanted to go to the desert with him.

CHAPTER TEN

IT REALLY WAS a wonderful, relaxing time.

In the morning Adele and Leila would swim gently and then lie on their backs in the healing water and talk.

Adele was now taking the tonic that the *attar* had prepared and she had never slept better. She was starting to awake refreshed, instead of wanting to pull the covers over her head and go back to sleep.

Sometimes she would see Zahir and they would walk on the beach or go for a drive.

They spoke about things but not about them, and though she ached to know if there was any progress or hope for them, she was also grateful that they didn't discuss it. It meant she could meet Leila's eyes when she returned.

One afternoon, as she and Zahir walked on the beach, Adele looked over at the glittering palace.

'How come it's called Diamond Palace when there are so many other stones?'

He didn't answer her.

'Zahir?'

'When you're ready to know, you shall.'

Zahir asked about the car accident she had been involved in.

'Did you see my notes?'

'Yes…' he nodded '…and also I heard Janet tell Helene.'

'I don't really like to talk about it.' If he could simply choose not to answer then so could she!

They walked in silence for a moment and she looked at the sparkling water and at the gorgeous palace ahead and wished she could stay here for ever.

It was Zahir who broke the silence.

'Do you know, I was going to buy you a car for helping my mother?'

Adele smiled. 'It wouldn't have been appreciated. I can't drive. I was only learning when it happened.'

'I could give you lessons,' he offered. 'I taught Dakan to drive when he first came to London. He's rather arrogant...'

'Like you.'

'Of course, and I doubted he would pay much attention to a driving instructor. I would be very patient with you, Adele.'

'I know you would,' she said, and she thought about it. He was very calm and controlled and if there was anyone who could teach her to drive it would be him, but she shook her head.

'After the accident I promised I would never get behind the wheel of a car again. I meant it. I just don't want to.'

'Fair enough.'

She liked it that he accepted her decision and didn't try to dissuade her.

And, Adele realised, she could tell him what had happened that day.

She wanted to.

For the first time she wanted to tell someone

who wasn't a lawyer or a police officer or an insurance representative.

'I'd only had a few lessons,' Adele said. 'I was on a main road and trying to turn into a street against oncoming traffic,' Adele said. 'I'd done it at the same spot the previous week, except this time it was rush hour and there was this wall of traffic coming towards me.'

She stopped walking and so did Zahir.

Adele couldn't both walk and talk as she recalled that day.

'I kept missing the gap in the traffic and realising afterwards that I should have gone then. I was starting to panic and the cars behind me were getting impatient and sounding their horns.'

He saw unshed tears but today he was grateful that they did not fall, for it might kill him to listen to this and watch her weep and do nothing. Given they were in view of the palace, he was very glad that Adele didn't cry as she told her tale.

'Mum suddenly said "Go…" and even as I went, even as I put my foot down, I knew that I'd made a terrible mistake. She said, "To hell!" and everything went slowly. I knew then that she had been telling the drivers who were sounding their horns to go to hell. I sent her there, though…'

'And yourself.'

Adele nodded.

'It was an accident, Adele. A terrible accident.'

'I know,' she agreed. 'And for the most part I've forgiven myself. I just…'

'Say it.'

She couldn't.

'You can say it to me,' he offered more gently.

'I think it would have been easier if she'd died.'

And she looked up into silver-grey eyes and they accepted her terrible truth.

'It would have been harder for you at first,' Zahir said, 'but, yes, easier on you in the end.'

'I don't know how to move on.'

'You already are,' he said. 'Moving on is just about going forward, not necessarily pulling away.'

And they started to walk again.

Slowly she started to heal.

The evenings were hers for relaxation and enjoyment and at night she would check on Leila's wounds and give her her tonic.

It was blissful.

A bliss Adele never wanted to end, but time was starting to run out and on her last Friday she and Leila lay on their backs in the salty sea water and Adele closed her eyes against the sun and just floated.

Leila was pensive beside her.

'My husband has to go on a royal visit to Ashla—a neighbouring country—tomorrow,' Leila said. 'I am thinking of joining him.'

Adele turned her head in the water. 'Will there be a lot of formal duties?'

'Not for me,' Leila said. 'Just one dinner on the Sunday night. I like visiting Ashla, we always have a nice time when we go there. We would return on Monday morning.'

That was when Adele flew home.

Her time here had raced by but now it was ending. Oh, it would be wonderful to see another country, but she loved her mornings in the healing baths and the occasional time spent with Zahir.

It was dawning on Adele that she might not see him after today and nothing had been solved.

Not a thing.

There was no solution.

'When would we leave?' Adele asked.

'Oh, no.' Leila shook her head. 'I do not need you to come with me. You can have the holiday you so deserve. I think a couple of days away with Fatiq are in order. Things are very strained between us.'

It was a huge admission and when Leila finally made it Adele gave it the attention it deserved and stood up in the water.

'Leila?'

'I love him very much. Today, though, is a difficult day and the build-up to it has been harder than usual.'

Adele remembered what had been said the afternoon Leila had collapsed. 'Is today Aafaq's birthday?' she checked, and Leila nodded, and then she too stood in the water and told Adele something that perhaps she should not.

Yet she could no longer hold it in.

'Things are very tense between Fatiq and me, Adele.'

'Birthdays and anniversaries are the worst. Well, I haven't lost a child and my mother's still alive but I know how much they hurt,' Adele said.

Indeed they did.

'Separate rooms aren't helping matters,' the Queen admitted.

'Does that have to be adhered to?' Adele gently enquired.

'I don't know.' Leila gave a helpless shake of her head.

'What about when you go away?'

'Oh, it will be separate apartments there,' Leila said. 'I cry every night.'

Adele was worried, not just for Leila but for Fatiq too.

They were grieving for their son but not together, and the rules kept them apart at a time when they needed to hold each other most.

And Leila spoke then about her tiny son, and how his little feet and toes had been just the same as his brothers. How hard he had fought to live. 'He wanted to live, just as much as I wanted him to live,' she said. 'I want his life to have meant something wonderful—instead, year by year, it is proving to be the death of our marriage.'

Adele didn't know what to say.

'Oh, we would never break up but we are growing further apart and this operation hasn't helped. Maybe I should have carried on with the healer.'

'Leila,' Adele said, 'you collapsed. And am I right in guessing that it wasn't the first time?'

'You are right.'

'You needed the surgery. I am so sorry you are hurting so badly today.'

'I will miss Aafaq for ever,' Leila told her.

'Of course you will.'

'It has helped to speak of him on his birthday. Usually I just deal with it alone and so does Fatiq. One day I hope we can speak of him but I can't see it happening. This evening Zahir is taking me to the desert so that I can visit Aafaq's grave. Usually I go by myself.'

'What about Fatiq?' Adele asked, and then corrected herself. 'I mean, the King. Does he go and visit the grave?'

'He went this morning.' Leila said. 'Alone. He's so…' Her face twisted in suppressed anger and Adele watched as she fought to check it.

'He's grieving,' Adele said. 'It manifests in different ways.'

There was a sad atmosphere back at the palace and, late afternoon, as Adele lay by the pool, she looked up and saw a helicopter. She guessed it was the Queen and Zahir.

It was.

He held his mother's hand as they were taken deep into the desert and he held her shoulders as she stood dry-eyed and pale at her son's grave.

Zahir looked at the small stone his father must have placed there earlier today.

'I wish we could celebrate his life,' Leila said. 'Yet all it does is tear us apart.'

Zahir knew his mother was referring to her marriage.

'Adele says that he is grieving,' Leila continued. 'That it manifests in different ways. I just thought he was angry with me.'

'He is grieving,' Zahir said, and he was glad that his mother had had Adele to talk to.

But soon she would be gone.

Now that he had seen a photo of Aafaq, now that he had spoken with his mother, it hurt even more to be here, and yet he would work through it.

Zahir prayed for his brother, for the tiny Prince who had never had a chance to serve his people.

He himself, on the other hand, did have a chance, yet it was being denied to him.

Still there was no hint of solutions.

He knelt in prayer and every fibre in his body strained for a sign, for a glimpse as to what he should do.

Be patient.

Do what is essential.

In time the answers will unfold.

Yet *still* they hadn't.

He picked up sand from his brother's grave and pocketed it.

And then he put his arm around his mother and walked her back to the helicopter.

She was drained and tired and Zahir was again glad that Adele was at the palace because she greeted the Queen with a gentle smile and he knew that his mother was in good hands.

Adele walked up the many stairs with Leila and on the way she saw Fatiq and lowered her head as she had been instructed to.

'Fatiq,' Leila called to her husband, and there was a plea in her voice. Adele would happily melt away if only these two would talk, would embrace, but then the King spoke.

'Layla sa y da.'

Goodnight.

Adele checked Leila's wounds and they had all healed. She gave her her potion and Leila lay in the vast bed and looked so alone.

'You're going to cry when I go, aren't you?' Adele said.

Leila nodded.

'Would you like to cry with me?'

And she did. She cried for her tiny son who should be a man and her husband who seemed to be moving further away from her every day.

And Zahir heard it.

Walking in the grounds, he heard his mother weeping and he wanted to go upstairs and shake his father.

There must be change.

He was no longer patient.

CHAPTER ELEVEN

LEILA SEEMED MUCH better in the morning.

'Look,' she said to Adele when she came in to check on her.

They would not go to the healing baths today as the King and Queen were flying off and Leila was preparing for her trip.

She held out a small square of fabric to Adele. 'I made this last night.'

There were tiny rows of gold and reds and above dark navy and dots of stars and there in the centre was a small silver heart.

'Where the earth and sky meet.' Adele smiled. 'For Aafaq.'

'It is beautiful, isn't it?' Leila said. 'I put all my love into it.'

Her maid came in to dress her and Adele witnessed a very regal Leila. She wore a cream gown

with a sash and when they went downstairs Fatiq
was wearing a military uniform.

All the staff lined up to formally bid them farewell as it was official business they were leaving on.

'I will be back on Monday morning,' Leila said
to Adele, 'in time to say goodbye. You are to
enjoy your days off. Do you have plans?'

'I want to go to the souqs and to see the desert,' Adele admitted.

'Well, there is a driver at your disposal, just
take some time for yourself.'

'You do the same,' Adele said.

Fatiq went to his office to say goodbye to his son.
'You are now ruling.'

'Not really,' Zahir said. 'If I make any changes
over the weekend, you will simply veto them on
your return.'

'Then don't make changes,' Fatiq said, and
turned to leave.

'Father…' Zahir called him back, not as a king

but as a father. 'Please go gently on my mother. She is recovering from surgery...'

'She is recovering from an unnecessary procedure. She left the palace laughing and smiling, yet she has returned unable to climb the stairs unaided and she weeps each night. Now, with the help of the *attar* and the healing baths, she is slowly starting to recover. It does little to enamour me to your modern ways. However, I do think, on my return, we could consider plans for a birthing suite at the hospital.'

It was the tiniest concession but a possible step forward.

Zahir didn't trust that it would transpire.

'As well as that,' the King said, 'I think we should hold the selection ceremony soon. I was going to invite Princess Kumu...'

'Don't extend any invitations,' Zahir said. 'Not without my consent, for it would not look good if Princess Kumu and her family came to the palace and I was not here.'

Zahir had fired a warning shot and he watched the clench of his father's jaw.

Yes, he was warning that he might leave.

The King did not respond to the threat from his son, just walked out of the office, and Zahir followed him.

They bade farewell and Zahir stood there as his parents were driven to the airstrip.

He watched them take off.

Zahir was now the ruler.

There was no point working on the hospital in his father's absence, he knew that.

Yet change would be implemented.

'Ask Adele to come and speak with me in my office,' Zahir said to Bashir, a royal aide.

His office looked out over the desert and he put his hand deep in his pocket and felt the sand he had taken from his brother's grave.

'You asked to see me?' Adele said, and the sound of her voice lifted his soul and he knew he was right to do what he was about to.

He nodded and turned.

'How about I show you the desert?'

'Is it allowed?'

'I am the ruler,' Zahir said. It didn't fully answer the question. 'If you want to call the nursing home and enquire about your mother, you should do so now, because there will be no reception out in the desert.'

'How long will we be there?'

Zahir didn't answer.

'Should I bring anything?'

'No.'

She called the nursing home and spoke to Annie. 'How is she?'

'She's the same. When are you back?'

'On Monday.' Adele hesitated. 'Annie, I'm going into the desert, I'm going to be out of range...'

And she thought of Zahir's words and she told herself that she was simply moving forward, not pulling away.

'We'll take care of her, Adele,' Annie said. 'You go and have a wonderful trip. Time in the desert, out of range, sounds magical to me.'

It was the most exciting adventure of her life.

Adele sat next to Zahir in the helicopter and

they put on headphones; she was lifted into the sky and for a moment felt as free as a bird.

The palace was on the edge of the desert and soon all that was beneath them were golden sands.

'It's amazing,' Adele said into her mouthpiece. 'Just miles and miles of nothing.'

'No,' Zahir said, 'there is so much more to see.'

She just drank it in but Zahir was right—there was more.

The helicopter hovered and descended and she looked down at the sand dunes and saw a caravan of camels and their long shadows. It was truly mind-blowing to think that in this huge expanse there were people surviving and going about their business.

They flew over vast canyons and then the helicopter hovered as Adele took in a sight she had never thought she would—a desert oasis.

It was the most wonderful thing she had ever seen.

'There is a hot spring there.' Zahir's voice came

through the headphones. 'Birds gather and drop seeds...'

It *was* magical.

Adele was starting to believe in magic again.

'And people live there?' she asked, because there was an array of white tents set beside the hot springs lake.

'That is the royal desert abode. Would you like to see it from the ground?'

She nodded.

The closer they got the more Adele's excitement grew.

The helicopter landed and they ran under the rotors but soon the sand gave way to a rich lush moss that surrounded the water.

It was nothing like she had ever seen or imagined.

She had thought the desert abode was a tent in the middle of nowhere; instead there were trees, delicate flowers and the lake was a dazzling azure.

It was paradise.

'Do you miss coming here when you're away?'

'I do,' Zahir admitted. 'I miss home all the time, but not the politics.'

There was a herd of white Arab horses and they were magnificent.

'Do you ride?' Zahir asked.

'Very well,' Adele said, and then laughed at her own joke. 'That's a lie. I've never even been on a horse.'

He pointed to a large tent by the lake and told her it was the royal one.

'So who lives in the other tents?'

'There are maids and the horsemen and a falconer.'

'Where's your harem?' Adele teased.

'Over there.' Zahir pointed as they walked towards the main tent. 'There is a tunnel from their tent that leads to the royal suite.'

'Are you serious?'

'Yes?'

'And do you…?'

'I came of age in the desert, Adele.'

She was sulking as they reached the royal abode. Or she was trying to, but it was so beautiful that she forgot to be cross as she removed her shoes. The floors were covered with Arabian rugs and the walls and ceilings were lined with cascading white silk.

She took out her phone and Zahir smiled.

'Are you so bored on our date that you are checking your phone? I don't think that's a good sign.'

'Did your mother tell you about my date with Paul?' Adele laughed. 'Well, I'm actually checking for reception.'

There was none.

And her phone didn't tell her the time either.

'There are no clocks...'

'We go by the sun and the stars,' Zahir explained. 'The main reason for coming here is to get away from all things modern. I agree with my father on that point. Here is for introspection and to seek guidance. It is a haven from the modern world.'

'It's actually quite freeing,' Adele admitted.

It was and she told him why.

'You know, I always have this knot of dread—

what if I miss a call and it's about my mother? The first thing I do is check my phone, yet while I've been here…' she shook her head unsure she could explain, '…it doesn't matter.'

'Tell me.'

'Well, I've always put off having a holiday. I convinced myself I'd panic all the time in case something happened and I couldn't get to her.'

'You know, if there was any change then I would get you straight home.'

'I know.' Adele nodded. 'But, rather than panicking, I've found…' She didn't know how best to explain it. 'I'm ten hours away at best. It's actually nice to know if something happens I won't have to deal with it. I now understand why people kept suggesting that I take a proper break.'

'Good for you.'

'Anything could happen,' Adele said, 'and we wouldn't know.'

And then she met his eyes and they told him that anything could happen and she wouldn't mind at all.

She wandered around. There was the royal

suite with cascades of crimson silk and on one wall a red velvet curtain. Above the bed was a velvet rope.

'I doubt that summons breakfast,' Adele said.

'It doesn't.'

'Does that ring in the harem?'

'It does,' Zahir said.

She was tempted to pull it just to see some sultry beauty come through the curtain.

Adele did so and Zahir smiled and put her out of her misery. 'The harem was disbanded before my parents married. I believe it was a condition she insisted upon when she attended the selection ceremony.'

And she remembered Leila tapping at her ruby and telling Adele that she had made demands of her own.

Now she understood the demands Leila had made had not been about keeping her in splendour.

'Good for her.' Adele smiled.

And she thought of Fatiq, who really loved his

wife. She just wished she could help there, but knew that there was nothing she could do.

A maid served them some tea and pastries and they sat on cushions. They were alone, finally alone, and she never wanted it to end. 'When do we have to go back?'

'When we choose to,' Zahir said. 'Would you like to go riding? It will be sunset soon. I can have them prepare a gentle horse.'

'That sounds amazing.'

It was.

They went on a slow walk along the dunes and a huge orange sun turned the sands and the sky to molten gold. The colours meant it was like being in the middle of a furnace, yet with the setting sun a soft wind circled them.

The sky darkened and the first stars started to appear as the air cooled. Adele wanted more of the desert.

She wanted more of Zahir.

'Will Leila know…' Adele asked '…if we stay here tonight?'

'The staff are discreet. It might eventually filter back but you will be long gone by then. But I think she will understand when I tell her I have feelings for you. Deep ones.' He was honest. 'I can barely get my father to agree to an X-ray machine, I very much doubt he would allow you to be my bride.'

'I could never leave my mother.'

'I know,' Zahir said. 'So for now all we have is this time.'

'For now?'

'I told you, I have asked the desert for a solution.'

Which didn't seem a lot to hang hope on, Adele thought.

Perhaps she'd sighed because Zahir looked at her and smiled.

They arrived back at the oasis and when she'd thought there could be no more surprises she watched the steam rise from the hot waters as it hit the cold night air.

'Do you want to go in?' Zahir asked.

Often, too often, Adele had wondered how it might happen—a kiss that grew out of hand, as had been the case on the plane, or he might sneak her to join him in the royal suite. Never had she envisaged the absolutely certain, almost calm way he dismounted and held out his hand to help her down.

And she knew this was it.

They had withheld and resisted but finally they were alone and there was nothing now that could stop them.

Though there was one thing perhaps, Adele thought as he lifted her down and for a slow, sensual moment her body slid over his.

If Adele told him this was her first time, she knew Zahir might well reconsider.

And she didn't want that.

He held her against him and she could feel that muscular body and the roughness of his robe.

'You're sure?' he checked.

'Very.'

He turned her around and undid the zipper of her robe and it slipped to the ground.

A nearly full moon lit them and Adele could feel his eyes on her as she took off her underwear.

'It's cold,' Adele said.

'Then get into the warm water.'

The water came up to her shoulders and she stood and watched Zahir undress.

First he removed the scabbard that held his sword and dropped it to the ground, and then he disrobed and removed the leather straps from his feet. And then as he stood and she saw that magnificent body fully naked he strode with purpose to the waterside. She wondered if perhaps she ought to tell him.

No.

She lay on her back in the water and gave him full view of her body, and as he stared down she parted her legs and she felt her stomach tighten as he stared.

It was too late to be shy, she decided, and she would never regret this magical night in the desert.

He joined her in the water and Adele stood. They faced each other for a moment and then he reached over and she slid through the water to the demand of his hands.

The air was cold above the water but their kiss was warm and deep and his beard was rough and sexy.

His hands were over her skin, feeling her breasts, cupping them, and then teasing her nipples. Then down to her waist and then to her buttocks. All this as her arms wrapped around his neck. His mouth was so beautiful and she explored it. The steam had made their faces damp and their mouths slid easily.

She could feel him nudging at her stomach and one hand moved from his neck just to hold him again.

He lifted her so that her legs wrapped around his waist and she could feel the nudge of him at her centre and held him there. It made her kiss him harder as his hand slid to her sex and he felt her warm and slick.

And then they stopped kissing and she stared deep into his eyes, and they were back to their first meeting.

Somehow they had known even then that they were meant to be.

Their kiss was deep and her body pliant. Her arms were loose enough around his neck that he could guide her.

He positioned himself, one hand at the base of her spine and the other around himself so he could take her fast and deep, and she now stared into his eyes.

No kissing.

Just watching and waiting for him.

Yet he did not slide inside her easily, as he had planned to.

Adele made throaty noise at the bliss of intimate pain.

And Zahir realised that this was her first time as he seared into her, and though she moaned in pain she ground down in acceptance.

She was tight and the pleasure for him was intense. He felt her mouth bite his shoulder and he held her hips and thrust in hard. He knew from her moans that she gladly suffered an erotic mix of pain and bliss.

He was not gentle, he was rough, delivering the pleasure that made her thighs shake and her calves ache as they gripped him.

Her cold mouth came up to his and her tense lips were on his as he took her ever more deeply.

He angled himself and she stiffened at the new sensations he aroused and then she moaned because he stroked her inside so exquisitely.

They were surrounded by stars; they were there when she looked up and they were reflected on the water as she rested her head on his shoulder as he took her faster. They were bathing in the sky, that was how it felt; they were two stars locked now in eternal orbit.

Adele felt the swell and the hot rush of him deep inside and he moved her as she pulsed around him.

They were sweating in the cold air and heat below and she took every drop he delivered and then he stilled her with his hands and they kissed until she again rested her head on his shoulder.

'Why didn't you tell me?' he asked, still inside her.

'You might have said no.'

Zahir shook his head. 'Never.'

CHAPTER TWELVE

'I HEAR ABOUT you going out on dates?'

They were back in the tent, lying on the opulent bed and still wet from the hot water. She could see the bruise her teeth had made on his shoulder and she felt sore but sated.

'Yes, I've had many first dates.' Adele smiled.

He didn't ask about her being on the Pill and she remembered telling him that she was when she'd been hit.

She knew she had missed taking a couple of them. When she had stayed overnight at the hospital and possibly the day after that she hadn't taken it.

There was no point saying anything yet, though.

There wasn't exactly a glut of pharmacies in Mamlakat Almas.

She would deal with that later.

Adele had everything she wanted in this moment and many more times throughout the night.

She came to his hand and he came to her mouth.

They spent the night making love rather than waste a moment sleeping. Together they made up for lost time.

But all too soon morning started to creep in.

Zahir pulled back a drape and he dressed in his robe and left the tent as Adele lay there, watching the stars disappear and the day invading in a glorious riot of yellows and pinks.

'We'll leave soon,' he said when he returned from wherever he had been.

She didn't want to leave.

She had never felt more at peace than here in the desert.

'Are you looking forward to going home tomorrow?' Zahir asked.

'I'm...' Adele couldn't answer. She wanted to see that her mother was okay but she wasn't looking forward to it as such. And she wanted to sort out where she lived. She loved her career but just couldn't quite envisage Zahir not being there.

No, she couldn't answer honestly because the truth was that she wanted to be here, sharing his bed.

He saved her from lying with a kiss but she could hear the maids setting up for breakfast in the lounge and she pulled back.

'Where did you go?' Adele asked.

'To visit my brother's grave. I always do when I am here. I finally spoke with my mother about all that happened.'

'That's good.'

'I can see now that she had pre-eclampsia,' Zahir said.

'I'm sorry that I couldn't tell you.'

'No, I respect that you didn't,' Zahir said. 'I know that you think my father must be mad but...'

'It must be so difficult for him,' Adele broke in.

Her response surprised Zahir but Adele had given it a lot of thought. 'The one time your mother stepped outside tradition he lost his son.'

He thought about that as Adele went to bathe. She came back pink and dressed in a silver robe and neither wanted to leave, so they lingered over breakfast.

She drank a lovely infusion of hot lemon and mint and they ate sweet cakes and he saw that she was holding back tears.

'It isn't over,' he said. 'We have tonight. You will be in my bed back at the palace.'

She shook her head.

'The staff aren't going to say anything. They are good people and we will be discreet. My parents won't find out for ages and I am fully prepared for that.'

It wasn't that so much that troubled her.

It was the next day when she went home.

CHAPTER THIRTEEN

FOR LEILA THE hope that a weekend break might help her marriage soon faded.

And being away from home had been more tiring than she had anticipated.

In the morning, unable to face another day and night smiling and being gracious, she asked Fatiq to make their excuses and to fly them home.

'That is impolite,' Fatiq told her.

'I don't care,' she said.

Leila was through with being polite.

Fatiq had strode into the palace, not best pleased.

'Inform Zahir that I am back.'

And Bashir knew, because whispers had swirled through the palace, that Zahir was not here and neither was Adele.

Neither was the pilot who had taken them into the desert yesterday afternoon.

'I believe that Zahir is out,' Bashir said.

'Where is he?' Fatiq demanded.

Bashir did not answer.

Leila certainly did not need to know where their son was—he was a man after all.

'I am going to have some tea and then lie down,' she said. 'Bashir, would you have Samina disturb Adele and ask her to come and see me.'

Leila had the most terrible headache and it had been a strained time away with Fatiq.

'Of course,' Bashir said.

Oh, they delayed and played for time, and by the time the Queen had taken some morning tea and was slowly climbing the stairs, Samina came to her with the answer.

'Your Highness, Adele is not in her wing.'

'Where is…?'

And the Queen stopped herself from asking the question when she saw the conflict in Samina's eyes.

'Actually, don't trouble Adele.' She knew. 'I gave her the weekend off.'

'Where is the nurse?' Fatiq was coming up the stairs behind his wife.

'She likes to walk on the beach,' Bashir said.

Poor Bashir did his best too.

But the King was no fool. He climbed the stairs right up to the turret and looked out at the splendid view and then came back down.

'Where is the Crown Prince?' Fatiq asked. 'He needs to be informed that I am back.'

Bashir was sweating and Samina's eyes were wide as he answered the King.

'I believe that Zahir has gone to the desert abode.'

'Fetch Queen Leila's nurse,' the King said in a voice that had even the little hummingbird hovering at the fountain falter.

Oh, Leila would not be getting her lie-down!

'You are dismissed for now,' she said to Bashir, rather than have him answer that Adele too was at the desert abode, and she followed her husband back down and into his office.

'He took her to the desert!' an enraged Fatiq said to his wife as soon as they were alone.

'Adele always said that she wanted to see it. Perhaps he is giving her a tour. There might have been a sandstorm.'

The King gave a derisive snort, which told Leila what he thought of that. 'The palace staff are embarrassed. Thanks to your nurse—'

'My nurse,' Leila interrupted, 'saved *me* from embarrassment.'

She was angry too but she was also conflicted. Zahir always kept to the rules.

Now, were it Dakan who was home she might have been better prepared for such goings-on.

But Zahir?

A short while later there was the sound of the helicopter and they stood at the window and watched it descend.

Leila watched the helicopter land on the lawn and saw Zahir and Adele disembark.

They were relaxed and laughing and there had been no sandstorm, neither had this been an innocent tour.

They were lovers, she could see that it was so, and so too could Fatiq.

And then Zahir must have seen the royal jet for he stilled and put a protective arm around Adele.

The King sucked in his breath at the public display of affection.

Leila watched as Adele startled and turned as if to run.

'My parents are here,' Zahir told her.

'They can't find out.'

He looked up at the office window.

They already have.' He took charge immediately. 'Come. We will go in by my private entrance and I shall take you this morning to the airport myself. You don't have to face them.'

Adele had never even set foot in his wing.

And now she sat on his bed with her head in her hands and she felt mortified.

'Can you say we got stranded, or that we slept apart…?'

'I'm not going to lie, Adele,' Zahir said. 'My only regret about what went on is that it now makes things difficult for you.'

'And impossible for us,' she said.

'Not necessarily.'

'Somehow I don't think there's going to be a solution here,' she said, and it was a jibe at the faith he had that things would turn around.

But he remained calm.

'Adele, it is better they know. Not yet, of course, but in the long run it is better than doing and saying nothing and marrying a neighbouring princess simply to appease him. I am not going to apologise for last night.'

His only regret was that Adele would be embarrassed and he would now do his best to handle that.

He left her on his bed and walked down the stairs towards his father's office. He nodded to Samina, who was crying, and he gave a small nod to Bashir. He knew they would have done their best to cover for him and Adele.

One of the guards gave him a small grim smile of quiet support as he opened the door and admitted Zahir to face a very angry king and a rather strained queen.

Zahir returned the guard's smile.

And then he stepped in and took charge.

'We shall speak later,' Zahir informed them by way of greeting. 'Right now I am going to take Adele to the airport. Clearly it will be uncomfortable for her to remain here.'

'You don't even try to hide it,' the King shouted in exasperation. 'You don't even attempt to come up with a polite excuse!'

Zahir's response was calm. 'I refuse to hide any more that I have feelings for Adele. I have been doing just that for the past year and it has got me nowhere. I have driven past her, drenched in a storm at a bus stop, and told myself I was right to do that, that it was essential to keep my emotions in check. I have ignored her, I have tried to remove myself from her and I refuse to do so any more.'

'You have free rein in England,' the King retorted angrily. 'And I know full well that you and Dakan use every inch of it. You know not to bring those ways here.' He looked at Leila and of course he now made it her fault. 'Now, if there were still a harem none of this would have happened…'

'This isn't about sex!' Zahir said.

And Leila blinked in confusion, not at what Zahir had just said but at his words before.

'Zahir, I don't understand,' she admitted. 'Why did you drive past her when she was drenched from a storm? I taught you better than that.'

He did not answer and Leila's heart broke for her son as she realised the reason was a love that could never be.

Never, because she looked at Fatiq and he had become a stranger.

'We shall leave by my private exit,' Zahir said to his father. 'There is no need for Adele to receive your disdain.'

He walked out.

'I expected better from Zahir,' Fatiq said.

'Why?' Leila retorted. 'He is his father's son. Remember how you used Bashir's ladder to come to me after the selection ceremony because you could not wait for the wedding night?'

The King said nothing.

'We had the biggest premature baby that this kingdom has ever seen,' Leila now shouted. 'Zahir's shoulders nearly killed me and we had to smile and pretend he was small.'

'At least we were betrothed.'

'Barely,' Leila snarled.

It had been the night of the selection ceremony that they had first made love and she had told him that night that if he wanted her then the harem was to be gone.

Fatiq had readily agreed.

They had known on sight they were in love, Leila thought.

Look at them now.

Oh, she ached for her son and Adele.

And she ached for herself and her husband too.

Zahir spoke with Samina and told her to pack Adele's things and then to arrange to have them put in his car. He told Bashir to move Adele's flight forward by a day.

Then he headed to his suite.

'Should I go down and apologise?' Adele asked.

'No,' he said. 'You have nothing to apologise for.'

'I'm her nurse!'

'Adele, we didn't exactly do it in a cupboard while she was breathing with the aid of a ventilator.'

That made her smile.

'No,' she admitted.

'You were on holiday by then and she was away in another country, trying to sort out the disaster of her own relationship while I was working on mine.'

And he acknowledged then to Adele that he knew the trouble his parents' marriage was in.

'He's so stubborn, so set in his ways...'

'You're not,' Adele said. She had thought Zahir was at first, but she had seen how open he was to discussion and change and how calm he was under pressure and she loved him so very much.

'I don't know how to help them,' Zahir said. 'Every time I bring up change he gets angrier...'

'Maybe he's scared to be proved wrong.'

Zahir dismissed that.

'He's not scared of anything. Come on,' he said. 'We shall leave by my private exit.'

Except it was not so easy to leave quietly.

Samina came and informed Zahir that the Queen had requested that the car be bought to the main entrance and that the Queen wished to bid farewell to Adele herself.

'Don't apologise,' Zahir told Adele again. 'Not just because you have done nothing wrong but because it would acknowledge that something occurred.'

He saw her frown.

And now he smiled.

'Just wish her well.'

Oh, Adele did.

She loved Leila very much; she was so much more than a patient to her.

If ever there was a walk of shame, though, this was one, Adele thought as she went down the palace steps with Zahir by her side.

The King was nowhere to be seen but a strained-looking Leila stood at the bottom of the stairs to say goodbye to her guest.

She was supposed to have helped her to feel better; instead, Adele could see the tension in her features and she could not meet her eyes.

'Zahir,' Leila said, 'perhaps you could wait for Adele in the car.'

Adele screwed her eyes closed and pressed her lips together because she wanted to say how sorry she was yet Zahir had told her not to apologise.

'Thank you for the care you have given to me,' Leila said.

Adele's cheeks were on fire and still she could not bring herself to meet the Queen's eyes.

'I am going to miss our lovely walk and talks,' Leila said.

'So am I,' Adele said. Oh, how she would!

'I have a small gift for you,' Leila told her, and her voice was a little shaky but she remained dignified as she handed Adele an intricately engraved wooden box. 'Please open it.'

'I don't think I deserve a gift,' Adele said.

'You do.'

'No,' Adele said, 'I don't.'

'How could I be cross with you for loving my

son?' Leila whispered, and then spoke in a clearer tone. 'Please accept my gift.'

Adele opened the box and was dazzled. A stunning sapphire that was beyond anything she had ever seen, let alone touched, was being given to her.

'It comes from the palace wall, from the same guest room where you stayed,' Leila explained. 'In a few weeks' time a ceremony will take place and the hole where your stone was will be filled with a diamond. One day, generations from now, the *qasr*, I mean the palace, will live up to its original name. The only requirement to accept this gift is discretion. We don't need the world to know or understand our ways. Adele, please accept it and I trust you to keep the spirit in which it was given.'

'I shall,' Adele said. 'Thank you.'

It was agony to get in the car.

Adele didn't want to go home, she simply didn't want to ever leave, but she climbed in and Zahir was silent as he drove off. He looked down at the box she held in her hands.

'You understand what the gift means?'

'I do.' Adele nodded. 'What happens in the palace stays in the palace.'

Zahir gave a small smile at her interpretation and nodded. 'Pretty much.'

Through dusty ancient streets he navigated the vehicle and she looked at the glittering city skyline that was so modern in comparison with the villages she had seen from the sky. And she remembered the comments she had read about Mamlakat Almas and the suggestion that it was best not to get sick here.

'I don't know how long I shall be,' Zahir said, 'but know this isn't the end.'

And she looked out of the car and at a city that needed a hospital and a modern health care system to be implemented. Zahir had a fight on his hands to do that.

'It has to be the end.'

'I know you don't share my faith but I have asked for a solution.'

'There isn't one.'

She would not cry when she said goodbye.

And she didn't.

'Can I ask that you don't call me?' Adele said.

'I need to know that you get home okay.'

'Well, turn on the news tonight and if there haven't been any plane crashes, you can assume that I did.'

'I will be back in London at some point.'

'And very possibly married.'

'No.'

'Zahir, you know there are going to be repercussions. This country needs to change and your father will use anything he has at his disposal and so will you…'

Would he?

Could he turn his back on Adele and take a wife if it meant better care for his people?

'I shall address things with my father.'

'Why?' Adele said. 'I can't come here. I'm not leaving my mother.' And it wasn't just that. 'After this morning I could never face your parents again.'

It was impossible, and safer to end it.

'I've had the most wonderful time of my life,' Adele said.

'I'll see you in London.'

'I shan't be your mistress, Zahir.'

'Liar.' He smiled. 'I might have to reinstate the harem and keep you there.'

How could he make her smile even now?

Yet he did.

There could be no kiss or embrace for they were in public and so she walked off and went straight through customs and she did not turn around.

And still she did not cry.

Not on the plane because it would be so loud that they would have had to divert to the nearest airport as she wailed.

And not even when she landed.

To terrible news.

CHAPTER FOURTEEN

LANDING IN LONDON, Adele told herself that she should be looking forward to seeing her mother; instead, she was resisting listening to a message that Zahir had left on her phone.

There was also one from the estate agent, informing her that the flat was hers.

That call she returned.

And then, before she went to the underground to take the tube home, she rang the nursing home and told them that she was home.

'Hi, Adele,' Annie said. 'We weren't expecting you back till tomorrow. How was your holiday?'

'It was wonderful, thank you,' Adele said. 'How's Mum?'

And she waited for the familiar answer— that she was comfortable and that there was no change. Instead there was a pause.

'You need to come in, Adele.'

No, her mother wasn't dead, but there was something that Annie needed to discuss and not over the phone.

Adele went straight there.

She didn't even stop to drop her suitcase back at the flat and she sat with it beside her in the nurses' office.

'When she had her hair washed last week, the nurse noticed a lump on her neck. We spoke with her GP and a biopsy was done. Adele, we did discuss telling you...'

'I understand why you didn't.' Adele said. She was grateful for the thought they had put into it. Of course she would have rushed back and for what? To sit by her mother's bed and await results.

She wouldn't have had the time with Zahir, even if it had come to such an embarrassing end.

'When do the results come in?'

'Dr Edwards expects to have them back tomorrow when he does his rounds.'

Adele sat by her mother's bed and held her hand.

'I'm back,' she said, but of course there was no response.

There never had been since day one.

And then, only then, did Adele allow herself the bliss of listening to Zahir's voice as she turned on the message he had left on her phone.

'Call me when you land,' he said in his lovely deep voice that felt like a caress. 'Let me know how you are.'

She didn't, because she needed him so much now and it would not be fair to tell him so, knowing there was nothing he could do.

No, she had no faith in the desert offering a solution.

And she sat by her mother's bed.

'Call me when you land… Let me know how you are.'

She played it over and over and over some more.

And the next day, after picking up the keys to her new home and signing the lease, she listened to it again before she went back to the nursing home for Dr Edwards's round.

'It isn't good news, Adele.'

He was terribly kind and as Adele sat in the office he gently explained that it would be wrong to send her mother for invasive tests and treatment.

Nature would take its course.

'I want her to have pain medication,' Adele said.

'Of course.'

'I want to be sure that she's not in any pain.'

'We'll do all we can to ensure she's comfortable.'

It was Adele who was the one in pain. There was a wash of guilty relief that finally there was an end in sight and that was so abhorrent to her that she was propelled to her feet.

'I'm going to go and sit with her,' she said.

And as she did she held her phone to her ear.

'Call me when you land,' Zahir said in his lovely deep voice that felt like a caress. 'Let me know how you are.'

Adele hit delete.

And then she gave her mother a kiss and headed

out to the office. 'Annie, I need to update my contact details.'

She had deleted his number and blocked him and by tomorrow she would be at a different address.

And the day after that she would be back at work.

'Wow!' Helene said as a suntanned Adele came into the changing room. 'How was Paris?'

'Fantastic.' Adele smiled.

'Good God, how hot was it?' Janet said as she took in Adele's sun-bleached hair and brown limbs.

'Pretty warm?'

'Are they having a heatwave?'

'I think they were.'

'Where's our postcard?' Janet checked.

'It must be on its way.'

She didn't tell them about her mother and she certainly didn't tell them she had been in Mamlakat Almas.

Instead she was brought up to date.

'Zahir didn't renew his contract,' Janet informed her as they walked around to the nurses' station, 'so we're rather short-staffed, though what's new?'

Everything, Adele thought.

The place felt different without him, though her home life was better, of course, now that she lived alone.

The days just seemed to limp by, though.

For Zahir they did too.

She had been gone almost a month and there was no progress that Zahir could see.

In any direction.

He was working with Nira, the architect, and she had some wonderful suggestions but his father just knocked back every one and it incensed Zahir.

'Why are you so opposed to this?' he demanded of the King.

'Our scholars are the basis of your system. We were the forerunners, and that wisdom I refuse to lose. I consult with the Bedouins and the elders, not with you.'

Zahir walked out.

His father was right. His culture had contributed so much to modern medicine. Surely they could marry ancient and modern. Other countries managed it and yet his father blocked him at every turn.

He found himself on the beach, and he strode in the pristine white sand and looked out to the stunning gulf and he did not know the solution.

He looked up at the palace and saw that a long ladder was resting against the wall that led to the suite where Adele had resided.

Up the ladder a man went, and beneath it were the elders, all watching as the small ceremony occurred.

From early times the elders, with little evidence, had believed that Mamlakat Almas was a land of diamonds. Rubies and other precious stones had been panned from the rivers and later mined. So convinced were they, despite evidence to the contrary, that the kingdom held the most precious stones, that when the palace had been built it had been named Diamond Palace. Its walls had been dotted with precious stones with the promise that one day diamonds would be discovered. They had been and now, when a guest stayed at the palace, they were presented with a stone from the wall and it was replaced with a diamond.

There were rare exceptions.

On the night of the selection ceremony the Sheikh Prince would meet with the elders and the King. A diamond would represent each bride and when the Sheikh Prince had made his selection he would hold the diamond in his palm and show his choice to the King. If the King endorsed the decision he would place his palm over the chosen stone and it would then be presented to the future bride.

That should be Adele's stone.

Zahir strode over, and his shout halted proceedings and he told them to hand over the stone.

Adele's stone.

The elders frowned and tried to argue with him but Zahir was having none of that.

'I am the Crown Prince of Mamlakat Almas,' he reminded them. Not that it counted for much as his father had the final word after all, but for now he put his hand on the hilt of his sword. 'You can take it up with him later, but for now you are to give me the stone.'

They did so.

He put it into his deep pocket.

He made his way back to the palace and he saw his mother sitting in the lounge, taking tea.

Leila was doing her sewing and, despite the tension in the palace, she was looking forward to tonight. It had been six weeks since her surgery and she and Fatiq had a romantic meal planned.

Maybe when they shared a bed again it would be easier to communicate and his mood would improve.

All was seemingly well and yet she could not relax. She looked up when she heard Zahir stride through.

'Zahir?'

'I am going into speak with the King.'

And her heart sank because she had dreaded

this moment and yet she had anticipated its arrival.

Two proud, immutable men, both of whom thought they were right.

And she loved them both.

The huge wooden doors to the study were closed and the guards were outside and she gave them a look that told them they had better not attempt to halt her.

One bowed and opened the door and she stepped into a heated exchange and listened as his son stated his case.

'Even the healer has opened his mind. He and the *attar* have liaised with Mr Oman and they have worked well together to return the Queen to full health.'

'She wouldn't have been so ill were it not for the surgeon. You have never had a day's ill health in your life,' the King again pointed out.

He refused to understand and Zahir shook his head.

'I will not sit back and do nothing. If you refuse to implement the changes I have suggested then

I am returning to London. At least in England I
can save lives. I will return when you either give
me the authority I need, or on your death…'

'Zahir,' Leila said in a shocked tone, and he
turned and looked at his mother.

'Tell me another choice,' Zahir said.

Leila had spent many nights awake, trying to
come up with one, and she gave a sad shake of
her head.

Zahir had not finished, though.

'I shall be taking this stone and asking Adele
to marry me.' He held out his palm to his father,
who should now place his palm over the stone,
in acceptance of Zahir's choice.

Fatiq did not.

'Adele would make a wonderful queen.' Zahir
fought for her, for them.

'She brings nothing,' Fatiq said.

'Adele was like a breath of fresh air to this palace,' Zahir countered. 'She has emotional char-
ity and that is a rare gift indeed.'

'I will never endorse that marriage.'

'Well, I don't need you to.' He did not look at

his father as he answered; instead, he turned to his mother when she asked him a question,

'You love her, don't you?'

'Very much,' Zahir said. 'And she loves me.'

The King had other ideas, though. 'Adele only wants you for your riches. She persists because...'

Zahir closed his eyes and still did not turn as he spoke.

'Adele does not persist. She has cut off all contact. She has blocked me from calling her. I had somebody go to her home but she has moved. Anyway, her mother is very sick so she cannot be here.'

'So this is just an excuse for you to turn your back on your people?' Fatiq said.

Leila addressed her husband then.

'Zahir has never made an excuse in his life,' Leila told him, and she gave her son a small smile.

'Is that why you did not stop for her when you were driving because you knew where it might lead?'

Not just bed, Zahir could have handled that. It had been more that it would lead to this.

To standing in his father's office and being told he could not marry the woman he loved.

'I loved her then,' he said to his mother.

'And is this love the reason you did not want her to come here and be my nurse?'

Zahir nodded. 'It was. But I have found out that she is essential to me.'

And they were the words from the desert.

Zahir was so angry at his father but as he went to walk out he remembered what Adele had said, and the sympathy she had shown for his father.

'I spoke to Adele about Aafaq,' Zahir told his mother and he saw her face flinch.

'I told Adele it was not to be discussed with you,' Leila said.

'She did not tell me anything. When I asked her a question she said I should speak with you, and I did. And when I visited my brother's grave, as I do every time I return to the desert, I again sought a solution. When I returned to the tent I said how angry I was about the health system here and how frustrated I was by the complete lack of progress. Adele said that she understood my father's plight.'

Now he turned around.

'This is not to be discussed,' the King warned.

'Then we won't discuss it,' Zahir said, 'but you will listen.'

'No, I saw what your machines did to my son.'

'They kept him alive till you got there,' Zahir said, and he now fought to be gentle for he could see his father's pain. 'My mother had a condition called pre-eclampsia. The only treatment is delivery. That is it. They can try to hold off delivery for a few days, but by the time she arrived at the hospital it was too late for that.'

'Zahir,' Leila said, 'please don't.'

'Yes,' Zahir said. 'He needs to hear this. Had she got there earlier they would have given my mother steroids in the hope of maturing the baby's lungs and they would have given her treatment to bring her blood pressure down to avoid her having a stroke. And though my mother cannot remember much more about what happened,

I know that had the pregnancy continued she would have had a stroke or a seizure. I know, from all I have studied, that had my mother been here she would have died. She would have been buried in the desert with her son in her womb. I *know* that. You would have lost them both,' Zahir said. 'You would have lost your Queen.'

'I don't believe that,' Fatiq said.

'Then I can't help my people. I shall return when my hands are untied.'

He put the stone into his pocket. He felt the sand from the desert and, as had been promised, yet not in neat order, the answers came to him.

He thought of Adele and what she had said, that maybe his father was scared to be wrong.

For if he was wrong, didn't that then mean his pride had killed his own son?

'Father, I don't believe modern medicine could have saved Aafaq back then. Maybe now, twenty-five years on, he might have stood a better chance. I have seen the photo of him, and from my mother's dates most babies born at that stage died back then.'

Fatiq said nothing.

'You could make Aafaq's death mean something. He could be the catalyst for change—'

'Go,' the King interrupted. 'Go to the woman who you put before your people.'

'If that is your opinion then you don't know me.'

Zahir was done.

Fatiq remained in his office, but Leila walked with her son to the royal jet.

'It had to be said,' Zahir told his mother, and he put his arm around her as they walked.

'I know it did,' Leila agreed. 'I have been trying to keep the peace and it has got us nowhere.'

'You'll come and see me in London?' Zahir checked.

'Of course I shall.' Leila smiled. 'Give my love to Adele.'

'I will.' He looked at his mother. 'You'll be okay?'

'Zahir, I am not scared of your father. The only thing I fear is that I have lost him. I love him so much. I am angry at his resistance to change, but now maybe I can see why he resists. Your father and I need to talk about Aafaq, and you need now to be with Adele.'

Zahir nodded.

He did.

Finally his patience had run out.

There was no answer, he could not fight for a solution any more.

He looked down at the desert as he flew over it. He wished he were down there, just for one more day.

There was so much guidance he needed and now he had his parents' marriage to add to an increasingly growing list.

And his upcoming marriage.

He reached into his robe and took out Adele's stone.

There was but one regret with Adele.

The night he had left her alone in a storm.

It had gone against everything he believed in.

How he wished he could take that night back.

And yet, would she have been ready for the strength of his desire?

At least then, by the time his mother had fainted, they might have faced the upcoming problems as a couple.

Then again, things had unfolded in time.

A word came to him.

Resolution.

There could be resolution at least for him and Adele.

He would focus on that for now.

CHAPTER FIFTEEN

ADELE SAT BY her mother's bed and held her hand.

The room was silent and, apart from the diagnosis, nothing had changed.

Yet everything had.

'You're going to be a grandmother,' Adele told Lorna. 'I found out this morning…'

She wanted to cry.

Yet she was scared to.

She was terrified to break down only to have no reaction from her mother. She was scared that Lorna might fail the final test Adele had set long ago—that desperate tears might awaken her.

She didn't want to know the answer and yet she couldn't hold it in any more.

She started to cry from the bottom of her soul and she rested her head on her mother's chest and held her hand as she wept.

There was no reaction from her mother, no arms went around Adele, and there was no attempt to reach out to her daughter in her plight, no tiny squeeze of her hand.

Adele lifted her head and watched her own tears splash on her mother's face and crying brought her no comfort.

None at all.

So she stopped.

'I'm going to be okay,' she said to her mum. 'I know that I shall be. It's good news really...'

It was.

A baby was good news.

Yet it was so scary too and she did not know how to tell Zahir.

She simply did not know.

It was a rainy summer day and she got off the bus and went into work to start her late shift.

The department felt different without Zahir there. It just did. Adele put her bag in her locker and closed it and then rested her head on the cool metal. She straightened up when Helene came in.

'I've lost my pen,' Helene said.

'Here.' Adele handed her one.

'How did Hayden do on his driving test?' she asked, because she had heard Helene saying he'd taken it yesterday but she had stopped talking when she'd seen Adele.

'He passed.'

'That's good.'

They had avoided the subject and sort of danced around it but Adele refused to play life like that any more.

And she was healing because as she walked around with Helene Adele felt her warped humour seeping back.

'Hey, Helene,' she said. 'Now that Hayden's passed, would you maybe give me some lessons?'

And she watched Helene's slight bulge of the eyes at the thought of Adele behind the wheel and then Adele laughed.

'You're wicked.' Helene smiled.

'I am.'

'Oh, by the way,' Helene said, 'Zahir called this morning. He wanted to speak to you.'

'Probably something about his mother.' Adele shrugged and feigned nonchalance but her cheeks went bright pink.

She couldn't hide for ever, but she did not want him calling her at work and if he did so again Adele would tell him not to.

Before or after she told him that she was pregnant?

Maybe she would be his London love after all, she thought.

She just could not see any other solution.

Zahir could.

To Dakan's utter shock.

Zahir had just come back from Admin, having signed a new six-month contract, and they sat in the canteen of the hospital and Dakan shook his head as Zahir spoke.

'You can deal with it if you so choose,' Zahir said. 'I have an architect lined up. Her name is Nira and you are to meet with her next week.' He looked at his brother's taut features. 'Or not.'

'Why not you?'

'I am tired of speaking with architects, only to have every suggestion they make knocked back by our father.' Then he told his brother what he had done. 'I will no longer be returning to cover any royal duties. Not until our father backs down. I have told him that that role now falls to you.'

'I have a life here.'

'Your duty is back there,' Zahir said calmly. 'I have always returned at short notice, but no more. You will now fill that role.'

'I never thought you would turn your back on our people,' Dakan said.

'And I never would,' Zahir replied. 'I shall rule when it is my time but until then it falls to you, or not…' He would wait this out, Zahir had decided. His silence and removal would hopefully force change. Dakan was the royal rebel, charming, funny and yet, Zahir knew, more than capable of filling the role of Crown Prince in his absence.

'You can't just swan in here, meet me for coffee and tell me…' Dakan started, but then halted as they heard the emergency chimes.

'Major incident. Could all emergency staff and the trauma team make their way to Emergency.'

It went on repeat and Zahir stood.

'You don't work here.'

'As of half an hour ago,' Zahir corrected him, 'I do.'

He strode down the corridor, and ambulances were already pulling up and patients were being wheeled in.

Most of them were crying children.

He headed straight into Resus, where Janet was busily setting up.

'What's coming in?'

'I'm not sure. We've been told it was a car versus school bus,' Janet explained. 'We haven't got a clear idea of the number of injuries or their severity yet, but given that it's a school bus I didn't want to wait and see.'

'Good call,' Zahir said as he put on a paper gown.

'You're back?'

'I just signed my contract. I'm fine to be here.'

Janet didn't really care right now whether or

not he had signed it. Zahir's hands were more than welcome, today especially.

The driver of the car arrived and she was extremely agitated and distressed,

'Try and stay calm,' Zahir said, but the woman kept crying and trying to sit up despite the fact she was wearing a hard cervical collar.

'Adele.' Janet called for Adele to come in and take over as she needed to be out there, triaging.

Adele walked into the resuscitation area and she saw him, his shoulders too wide for the paper gown. He looked up and just for a second their eyes met and this time he smiled and greeted her.

'Adele.'

And she wanted to run to him, to ask how and why he was there, but right now the patient was the priority and required all her attention.

The rest would all simply have to wait.

'I don't know what happened...' The driver was sobbing. 'A school bus. Oh, my God—oh, my God...'

'You're going to be okay,' Adele told her, and asked her name.

'Esther!' she said through chattering teeth, but it was an irrelevant detail to her right now. 'How badly are they hurt?' she begged. 'Please tell me how many are hurt?'

'We don't have that information, Esther,' Adele said. 'We're taking care of you.' She started to undress the woman. 'Zahir…' Adele said as she undid Esther's jeans.

Esther had wet herself.

'Can you open your mouth for me?' Zahir said, and he shone a torch inside. 'She has bitten her tongue. Esther?' he said in that lovely calm voice. 'Do you suffer with seizures?'

'No,' Esther said. 'Please can someone find out how many are hurt…?' And then she stopped begging for information and gave an odd, terrified scream, which Zahir recognised. Patients often experienced an aura before a seizure. It might be a terrible smell, at other times a feeling of impending death and fear, and often they let out a scream as they dropped, though Esther was already lying down.

'Help me roll her onto her side,' Zahir said.

And they did just that as Esther started to seize.

They hadn't worked together often, Zahir had made sure of that, but he found out now that they worked together very well.

He suctioned the airway as Adele pulled up drugs and soon Esther was postictal and snoring loudly while being closely watched.

And information was starting to emerge.

Paul, the paramedic, came in.

'We've just brought in the passenger. Apparently she and Esther were chatting when she let out a scream and started to fit.'

'Thank you,' Zahir said.

And other information was revealed.

He saw a worried look on Adele's face when the radiographer stated the usual—that if anyone was pregnant they should step outside.

And he thought of a night in a desert and of the magic the desert had made, whether you believed or not, and of course there might be consequences.

'Adele,' he said. 'I'll stay with Esther.'

Zahir was here and though there was no time

to catch up or to ask how or why, her world just felt better knowing he was near.

And later, Adele sat with Esther, who was awake now, distressed and crying.

'I don't know what happened,' she said. 'I need to know how the children are.'

'I honestly don't know,' Adele said. It was the truth. Janet had said she was to stay with Esther. She hadn't sought information; truly it was easier not to know what was going on than to have to withhold it from her patient.

It sounded as if the department was calming down.

There had been the sounds of crying and frantic parents arriving but the only person who had been bought into Resus since Esther's admission was a cardiac patient not related to the accident.

It could be good, or there could be other hospitals dealing with injuries.

For now, Adele focused on Esther.

Her toxicology screen was back. It would seem no drugs and certainly no alcohol had been involved.

Sometimes accidents happened.

Terrible, terrible things happened and there wasn't always someone to hang the blame on.

Except ourselves.

She thought of Fatiq and was quite certain now that he blamed himself for the death of his son.

For years she had beaten herself up over what had happened with her mother.

Now she ached for Esther.

One of the security guards called out that the news cameras had arrived and Esther closed her eyes in dread and fear.

'I can't face this…'

'You can,' Adele said.

She had.

Adele remembered seeing the images of her accident on the evening news as she'd sat waiting to find out if her mother would make it through surgery.

'Four members of a family have been taken to hospital and another woman is in a critical condition after a learner driver…'

Adele went with Esther while she had an EEG

and she sat with her for a long time until finally she fell asleep.

Janet left her alone.

She was a healer too and knew Adele needed this.

Later, much later, Adele heard the sounds of police radios and them asking Zahir if they could speak with the driver now.

'Adele.' Janet put her head around the curtain.

'It's time to go home.'

Adele shook her head.

'Yes, Adele, it's time to go home.'

Esther opened her eyes as Adele stood.

'I have to leave now,' Adele said. 'But I'll come and see you in the morning.'

Moving forward didn't necessarily mean pulling away.

Whatever the outcome.

Tomorrow Esther would know a friendly face.

CHAPTER SIXTEEN

ADELE STOOD IN the summer rain at the bus stop
and waited.

Not for the bus.

She let two go past.

It was like standing in a warm shower and she
was drenched right down to her underwear.

But finally she saw his silver car indicate and
turn and Zahir drove towards her. She hung off
the bus stop and swung her bag.

She saw the whiteness of his smile and then
he slowed down and stopped. The window slid
down and she walked over and stood there.

'Get in.' he said, as he had wanted to for so
long.

She lowered her head and peered into his lovely
plush car and then at the lovely, sultry man.

'You might not be able to afford me,' Adele said.

'Get in,' he said again.

She did.

And the world, and all that was going on in it, could wait for now.

This was about them.

About two stars who belonged, who connected, and together they shone brighter.

She was soaking wet and her clothes clung to her and he undid his seat belt and kissed her hard against the soft leather.

She dripped water all over him and the windows steamed up.

His hands roamed over her breasts and went up her wet skirt and between her legs. Then he peeled her wet body from his and started the car.

'That's what would have happened had I stopped that night.'

'Pity you didn't,' she retorted.

They drove through wet streets and the air was thick and potent. She asked no questions so he could tell her no lies.

Adele didn't want to know about the palace just

yet and she didn't want to speak of her mum, or find out about Esther.

Tonight had been waiting so long.

And he asked no questions either.

Zahir had only one thing on his mind.

She discovered his home was a very plush apartment and she sat in the passenger seat as he got out. She wondered how he might have explained her arrival that wet, stormy night.

Zahir, she soon found out, explained himself to no one.

He greeted the doorman and told him that the keys were in the ignition and would he please park his car. He walked a very bedraggled Adele through the foyer.

There was another couple in the lift, and he wished them goodnight as they got out at the fifth floor. He pressed the button again for the eighth floor, the only sign of his impatience for he had pressed it once already.

He opened the door to his apartment but as they stepped in he asked but one question.

'Would you still be here now had I stopped the car that night?'

He deserved an honest response.

'I'd have been on my knees by now.'

For being so crude she was hauled over his shoulder and marched through his apartment and thrown onto his vast bed.

He removed her knickers and skirt and kissed her up her thigh with a rough unshaven jaw. Adele dealt with her top half herself. He kissed her very deeply, and there were a couple of fingers there too as he explored her intimately and so *thoroughly* that her feet pressed into his shoulders.

And she thought of that night and that he had not stopped and she shouted it this time.

'Pity you didn't,' she sobbed.

He kissed her again and when she came to his mouth he made her his again, and not gently.

Jacket on, tie on, he just unbuckled and unzipped and took her hard. He was fully dressed, she was naked and it was utterly divine.

There was not a thought in her head except how

she loved this man and how the world could disappear when it was just them.

Zahir got up on his elbows and thrust faster and she moaned and held his face in her hands, just because she had to. His hips thrust harder and he moved into that delicious point of no return and she watched his grimace and felt the rush of his release. She was rigid to the very soles of her feet as she came.

He did not collapse onto her afterwards, he just stared deep into her eyes. Sometimes she felt as if he was looking deep into her soul.

He was.

There was pain there still, but there was the shine of fresh happiness and a little ray of hope.

And he would make it grow.

'You haven't paid me,' she teased as he stood and zipped up.

'Here.' He went in his pocket and tossed her a diamond. If it had come from anyone other than Zahir she would have known it was false.

She slipped between the covers and sat there examining it, too stunned for words. He went out for a few moments and returned with two very welcome mugs of coffee.

'I really am getting the royal treatment,' she said, as he put a mug down by what was now her side of the bed and he undressed and joined her in it.

'We're getting married,' Zahir said.

'Has your father given his permission?'

He shook his head.

'We can't, then…'

'We can. I'm going to be here with you in England. I've signed a new contract.'

'No…' It was Adele who now shook her head. 'You belong there.'

'And one day I shall be, but for now I will do what I must do and that is to marry you. I can't live in a jewelled palace and live a charmed life when I cannot help my people. I shall return when I am able to do so and I hope that when I return it will be with you as my Queen.'

It had become, to Zahir, as simple as that.

He would do what he felt was essential and

trust that patience would serve him well and that the answers would unfold in time.

'Dakan can fill in for me until then. I am prepared to wait it out. I was speaking to him at the hospital today just as the alert came. He's not best pleased.'

And the rest of the world trickled in.

'How's Esther?'

'She's doing well. It would seem it was her first epileptic seizure. Thankfully there was no one seriously injured...'

He watched as she closed her eyes in relief and knew that today would have brought up a lot for her.

'How is your mother?' he asked, and he expected to hear that there had been no change.

'She's dying,' Adele told him. 'And please don't say sorry because I don't deserve it. To be honest, I feel a bit relieved.'

It was the most terrible admission and she felt his hand take hers.

'Who do you feel relieved for?'

'Myself,' and then she thought harder. 'I feel

relieved for her too. She's had no life since the accident.'

He took her in his arms and his hand explored her flat stomach. It was wonderful to think there was a life starting in there.

'Did you tell your mother she was going to be a grandmother?'

'How do you know?' She turned in his arms. 'I think I forgot to take my Pill when I got hit—'

'Adele,' he interrupted, 'I took you to the fertile waters by the royal tent...' He smiled. 'No Pill was going to save you.'

'Were you trying to get me pregnant?'

'Truth?' He looked at her. 'That night there was nothing on my mind but you.' He kissed her long and slow. 'But, yes, in taking you to the desert I knew one way or other that it would bring things to a head.'

'You're okay with it.'

'I am thrilled,' he said, and he kissed her again.

'Did I tell you how much I love you?' he asked. 'And how much I always will?'

He didn't have to.

She already knew.

Zahir took the stone and held it in his palm. 'In my country, when the choice is made, the Prince holds the chosen diamond in his palm. The King is supposed to place his palm over the stone.' He held out his hand. 'I don't need his acceptance, Adele, just yours.'

It was overwhelming.

Centuries of tradition she could wipe away with a sweep of her hand. But then she looked from the stone into his silver-grey eyes.

Zahir was better than that. Even now, loving her, he was preparing to one day return to his people, but with her by his side.

'I thought the desert hated me when I arrived,' Adele admitted. 'I felt, if it found out about us...'

'We made love in the desert, Adele, and it has given us the greatest gift.'

She looked up and smiled.

'I'm not just talking about the baby, Adele. We returned and we were caught, yet our night together confirmed our love. There's no need to be scared for the future.'

She wasn't now.

There was hope and there was excitement and there was a love that had proved to be undeniable so she lifted her hand and placed her palm over Zahir's.

They were together now.

'You don't belong on the palace wall.' He told her what he had been thinking that day as they had walked on the beach. 'You belong on the inside, as my Queen.'

And one day you will be, Zahir hoped.

CHAPTER SEVENTEEN

IT WAS TO be the tiniest of weddings.

The staff at the nursing home would be their witnesses and Adele and Zahir would marry by Lorna's bedside.

When Zahir made a decision, it was made, and he wanted Adele as his wife. The problems that the marriage might create he would deal with in the fullness of time.

Right now all he wanted was for their union to be official.

He had informed his father, who had terminated the call, as Zahir had expected him to. The formal invitation that Zahir had had delivered to the palace would have been torn up, he was quite sure.

He pulled up outside the nursing home at ten to two in the afternoon and was told by a smiling Annie that Adele wouldn't be long and that the photographer was already there.

They had worked so hard to ensure that even though this wedding was small it was beautiful.

Lorna's hair was back to brunette and her nails had been done and she was wearing a gorgeous nightdress. The room was decorated with flowers and after the brief service there would a lavish meal for the nursing-home staff and guests.

And, whatever the consequences, it would be done.

As was right.

'Lorna's ready to be mother of the bride,' Annie said.

'Could I speak with her, please?' Zahir asked, and Annie nodded and pulled the curtains around them.

Zahir sat down by Lorna's bed. He understood how poor her condition was yet he understood Adele a little better because he spoke to Lorna as if she could hear him.

Just in case she could.

'Today I am marrying Adele,' Zahir said. 'I

know that you must have your reservations, as at some point I will be a king and there will be many demands on both myself and Adele. I want you to know that I will do everything I can to support your daughter with that transition. I know that she will be a wonderful queen. I want you to know that I am not taking her from you. You need your daughter now and Adele needs to be here with you. We are so looking forward to the baby's arrival. Know that I shall take the best care of them.'

And Zahir understood Adele a little better still.

There was no response, no flicker of the eyes, no squeeze of the hand to say that she understood.

Poor Adele, Zahir thought, and poor Lorna.

'You have my word that I shall take care of her,' Zahir said.

And his word was worth a lot.

He came out from behind the curtains and startled, for there, instead of his bride, stood two very unexpected guests.

His mother and father had come.

Not to protest, Zahir quickly realised, for his father was wearing a suit and his mother embraced him.

They had heard all that he had just said to Lorna.

'Adele is pregnant! That is so wonderful!' Leila was beaming and always she surprised Zahir, because in her own way she fought for change. Her acceptance of the news made her husband step forward and shake his son's hand.

'We want to show that you have our support,' the King explained. 'And you do.' The King looked at his son. 'It is time for change.'

He had waited so many years to hear those words yet right now Adele was his top priority.

'I cannot come back just yet,' Zahir explained. 'Adele's mother is very ill.'

'We heard. Tomorrow an announcement will go out that you have married and that there will be a formal celebration back home, when the time is right...' Leila said.

'Who is in residence?' Zahir frowned, because

his mind never moved far from duty. 'Is Bashir acting…?'

'No, Dakan is in residence,' Leila said. 'And he has full rule. Your father and I are taking a holiday together. Our first… I remember saying to Adele that I hadn't had one.'

And then Leila stopped talking as the bride arrived.

She wore a slip dress in pale ivory and flat shoes, and she was carrying a bunch of jasmine that Zahir had had sent for her from his home. She was a bride fit for a king.

'Leila!' Adele said. 'Fatiq!'

Oh, she broke with protocol, she was so grateful to them for being here.

Her eyes filled with tears as Leila embraced her and congratulated her on the wonderful news that she was expecting a baby and Fatiq, handsome in a suit, smiled too.

'I hope it's a girl,' Leila said. 'A boy would be wonderful but I love to shop for girls.

And, in her own unique way, Leila had re-

moved any pressure on Adele to produce a suitable heir.

'Our people will be very surprised,' Leila said,
'but they will be happy.'

'Our people will be surprised too,' Adele said,
and Zahir smiled.

They hadn't told anyone at work.

That news would be shared on Monday and she
could not wait to see Janet's expression when she
explained the need for a new name badge.

Yet she wouldn't have to wait, for there were
two more guests at this very special wedding.

Janet and Helene, dressed to the nines, had just
arrived too.

'They worked it out,' Zahir said.

'Of course we did.' Janet smiled at Adele. Then
she went to see Lorna, who she had nursed on
such a black day.

Leila clapped her hands to get things under
way. 'I have brought a gift for your mother, and
also something that you should wear on your
wedding day,' Leila said. 'There are certain traditions that must be upheld.'

And it would seem there was going to be a delay, as the bride, according to Queen Leila, was not quite ready.

Adele went back, with the Queen, to the room she had dressed in.

'I can't believe that you're here,' Adele said, as Leila took out a sheer veil and started to arrange it.

'I can,' Leila answered. 'Believe me, Adele, I choose my battles wisely.'

'Battles?'

'There are some advantages to being a queen. When I get angry, I get very, very angry, and I told Fatiq that things were finally changing, that I never thought that I would see the day that I was absent from my son's wedding, that I had played by the rules but no more, that I had collapsed and still he would not consider a modern health system.'

'And he listened?'

'Not at first,' Leila said.

'But Zahir had spoken to him about Aafaq. Adele, he blamed himself, he was holding onto so much guilt and grief. We cried together for the first time and I think he came to understand that he would have lost us both and it was not his fault that Aafaq died. But, Adele, he is a very proud man—he had to be the one to make the decision and yet he is stubborn. I wanted my family to be together again so I decided to move things along.' Leila smiled a secret smile. 'Do you want to be my nurse for two more minutes?'

Adele frowned.

'You said I could confide in my nurse.'

'I'd love to be your nurse for two more minutes.' Adele smiled.

Leila nodded. She would say this once and once only. 'The day Zahir left was six weeks after my surgery. We had a romantic dinner planned but of course I was very upset that night. Well, six weeks turned into seven...'

Adele let out a gurgle of laughter.

'And if you ever say that to Zahir...'

'Oh, I never shall,' Adele said.

'Well, Fatiq asked if there was anything I could think of that might help me to feel better. I had just turned to my sewing and remained in my own room at night. I said perhaps a cruise, some time away, and that maybe a little romance might help me to return to my once happy self. But, of course, Zahir had gone and Dakan said he would only step in if he had free rein with the hospital. And then seven weeks turned to eight and the King suggested that maybe Dakan should take over, maybe a new system was in order! It had to be his idea, of course.' Leila rolled her eyes and then smiled. 'And now here we are and we are about to take a long overdue honeymoon!'

Adele was delighted. Leila had gone on a sex strike, and it was perhaps the funniest thing she had ever heard.

'You are no longer my nurse now,' Leila warned.

There would be no more confiding but Adele felt as light as a feather as she set to join a wonderful family, one with a very powerful queen!

Leila laughed too but then she became serious.

'I will do all I can to guide you too,' she said. 'I have never had a daughter and my mother did little to prepare me for the role. I shall not let that happen to you.'

It meant so much to hear that.

'Are you going on honeymoon too?' Leila asked.

'Not yet,' Adele said. 'I don't have any annual leave until September and Zahir has only just come back, but anyway…'

'You have this time with your mother,' Leila said. 'I have a gift for her. One thing you must understand is that when a favour is done or something precious is given…' She faltered. 'You are a precious gift to our family, Adele.'

'I see,' Adele said, though she didn't.

Leila left her then and Adele took a moment to breathe.

Their parents were here, together, to witness this day, and she felt as if the earth had moved just for her. And her friends were here too.

She walked out and her eyes should have first gone to Zahir but they were drawn to her mother's bed. The quilt that Leila had been working on for so many years, each stitch created with love, was over her mother's bed. The gorgeous silks, the complex beauty, and Adele knew that Lorna was wrapped in love for ever.

Adele wore a veil when she hadn't expected to and as she stood before Zahir and he pulled it back, her smile was wide.

There was love and peace in this room and she felt it all around.

She looked into Zahir's eyes as he made his vows in English. He more than met her gaze now.

He held it and it felt like a caress as he told her he loved her.

'I will do all I can to provide for your heart and to hold your trust as we share the journey ahead.'

He looked deep in her eyes and saw there was still pain, but he was patient and would work to see it lessen.

And Adele made her vows to him.

'You made me believe in love at first sight.' She believed in magic too now, for how could she not? 'I have and always shall love you.'

And that was it. They were husband and wife and Zahir, very thoroughly, kissed his bride.

They posed for official portraits and Adele knew they were important ones. Without the King smiling at their side, it would have sent a message of disapproval to his people.

Oh, Fatiq smiled beside his wife.

They were *finally* off on their honeymoon tonight!

There was a little party afterwards, and the oldies put on some music. Annie had hung up a disco ball so that light bounced off the walls.

Janet and Helene sat on Lorna's bed and told her about the magic being made.

The King and Queen were dancing dreamily, and a few of the residents too.

And, of course, Adele and Zahir danced.

The lights flickered and they felt again as if they were bathing in the sky.

Two stars locked in eternal orbit.

They were simply meant to be.

EPILOGUE

LORNA HAD DIED soon after the wedding.

There was no sense of relief for Adele.

She didn't even know how to cry.

Lorna had been buried wrapped in the blanket but still Adele had not been able to cry.

A month later they had returned to Mamlakat Almas for a formal celeration to mark their marriage and then come back to London so that Zahir could complete his contract.

The baby would be born in England.

When Adele was six months pregnant they went back for a flying visit. Even though they would be there for just one night, Zahir had made sure that there was the necessary equipment and staff on hand should something happen.

It was supposed to be a brief visit, a duty visit,

but just before they returned to the UK Adele had finally broken down.

This time, she had arms to hold her as she cried, but not with remorse or guilt. She simply wept for the mother she had lost.

It has been a long time coming and the grief did not fade with her tears.

The flight was delayed, of course, and Adele lay on their bed and tried to fathom that she was going to be a mother and that hers was gone.

Zahir was patient.

Yet his concern was deep and so was his love.

The *attar* prescribed a blend of herbs to nurture both baby and mother and also a slight calmative, and that helped a little.

On the morning that they were due to fly back to London they lay in bed and Zahir stared out at the desert, feeling the kicks of their baby beneath his hand when Adele stirred.

'Adele,' Zahir asked, 'are you looking forward to going home?'

Half-asleep, she answered him honestly.

'This is home.'

She loved England and would always go back to visit friends but Mamlakat Almas felt like home.

She stretched and turned to face him and, more awake now, she smiled, still unable to believe that she could wake up with him every morning. 'What time do we leave?'

And Zahir had come to a decision—the choice would be Adele's.

Dakan had moved mountains, his goal to get the birthing suite ready should Adele need it.

Zahir could feel how much more relaxed she was here.

'Do you want to stay?'

'Stay?' Adele checked. The baby was due in eight weeks and soon it would be too late to fly.

'Maja is a good obstetrician, she is one of the best...'

Dakan had made sure of that and Zahir would not even consider it if he did not trust Maja.

'We could have the baby here?' Adele checked.

'If that is what you want,' he agreed.

And Adele thought about it and realised she very much did.

It was the most wonderful time. Mornings were spent in the healing baths with Leila.

They spoke about Aafaq, yet Adele still couldn't speak about Lorna. Sometimes they just floated in silence. Adele, who had been without a mother for so long, loved that she had guidance and support from Leila.

Afternoons she would walk barefoot on the sands with Zahir and at night she would lie in his arms and try to comprehend how far they had come.

It was peaceful, it was gentle, it was bliss.

And then, two weeks before her due date, Adele woke up and looked out at a red desert sky.

'What time is Maja coming to see you?' Zahir asked.

'At midday,' Adele answered, but then she asked him something. 'Do you think she knew I was having a baby?'

All those hours, all the years talking to her mother without so much as a sign that Lorna could hear and yet she asked him now.

'I do.'

'You're just saying that.'

'No.' Zahir shook his head. 'Did you tell her about me...?'

'You were all I spoke about for a year.' Adele gave a soft laugh but then it changed. 'I miss that.'

It had seemed agony at the time but Adele now missed those times with her mum.

'Of course you do,' he said. 'I spoke to her on our wedding day and just like you had said there was no response, no sign she understood, yet she held on until she knew you were okay...'

'I don't know.'

Adele didn't know what to think.

'Talk to her again,' Zahir said. 'Maybe in your head. Have those conversations that you miss.'

Adele did.

She walked on the beach and in her head she chatted to her mum and told her how much she loved her.

How sorry she was.

And some tears fell and then she smiled. 'You'll be pleased to know I have a driver now.'

Zahir was right.

It helped to talk to her mother again. For years there had been no response but now she could feel the breeze on her face and the sand at her feet and she could talk to her whenever she wanted to.

Then Adele saw Leila walking towards her and she always made her smile.

Leila had nearly finished the blanket for the baby.

It was complete, save for one square, and she was trying to squeeze the baby's name out of Adele.

Adele wasn't telling; instead, they chatted about Maja's visit today.

'She thinks it might be wise if I deliver soon, given that the baby is so big.'

'Good,' Leila said. 'Hopefully you will be prescribed more time in the healing baths after you have the baby. I was there for weeks afterwards. You know how I suffered in my labours. Both Zahir's and Dakan's shoulders…' And then she hesitated but a little too late, for Adele had frowned.

'I thought that Zahir was premature?'

'He had very big shoulders,' Leila said quickly. 'Even at seven months.'

Then she looked up at the palace and saw the ladder against the wall and she smiled at the memory of Fatiq climbing up it to be by her side.

'This is the stone I received the night after the bridal selection,' Leila said, and she pointed to the ruby that she wore around her neck for Adele to admire.

And she gave a tiny, almost imperceptible wink.

Yes, what happened in the palace stayed in the palace, but those last tweaks of regret about her walk of shame left Adele then as she realised she that Zahir hadn't been premature in the least.

They laughed.

Zahir was working in his office when he took a moment to enjoy the lovely view and saw his mother and Adele walking on the beach.

He loved his country.

Always.

And he loved the changes that had been made and the care that had been taken of Adele. He could see her calm and relaxed and happy and walking with his mother.

He watched as Adele and his mother stopped walking and started to laugh.

Adele was doubled over with laughing and it was nice to see.

Leila carried on walking and talking and then turned as Adele failed to catch up.

He watched his mother walk back towards Adele.

That was all Zahir saw.

He swiftly made his way through the palace and down to the beach.

'I'm here,' he said, and then he stopped talking as Adele looked up and smiled in relief.

They shared a gentle kiss on the beach where she had first told him all that had happened and as they looked at each other he could see in her shining eyes the healing that had taken place.

And he knew then that they had been right to stay.

Samina helped Adele into a fresh gown and Zahir walked her down the palace stairs. When she bent over midway, Adele remembered the glare that had passed between father and son when Leila had doubled over.

Things were so different now.

The birthing centre was beautiful and the bliss of an epidural could not be overstated.

'Adele,' Maja told her, 'you need to have a Caesarean.'

She had come to realise that and so too had Adele and Zahir after a lot of very unproductive pushing.

It had always been a real possibility.

Adele was slight and Zahir was not and this was rather a large baby.

She thought of Queen Leila and what she had gone through and was so grateful for all that had changed.

Adele stared at the ceiling as she was moved through to the theatre and Zahir was by her side.

'The staff are praying for a calm and wonderful delivery,' a nurse explained, 'and then they will come in.'

Their ways really were beautiful, Adele thought.

Zahir was utterly calm and sat by her head and held her hand. He chatted as if they were sitting at a bus stop, rather than about to become first-time parents.

He calmed her in a way no one else ever could.

And she loved his patience and also his occasional impatience when a solution wasn't forthcoming at his pace and he pushed things along.

She loved his almost unwavering belief that the answers would unfold in time.

And she loved, most of all, how essential she was to him.

As he was to her.

It was a moment like no other.

She heard the gurgle of the suction machine and felt the odd sensation of tugging and then heard the sound of tears.

Lusty, healthy tears and they were gifted with a small glimpse of their son.

He had thick black hair and was a big, angry baby indeed. Adele laughed when she saw him and knew, as fact, the Caesarean had been necessary.

'Go over to him,' Adele said to Zahir, and he gave her a kiss and then did so.

The staff were a little nervous as Zahir approached.

He was not only a doctor but would one day be king and so too would his new son.

'He is beautiful, Your Highness,' Maja said. It was the proudest moment in her career to have delivered the future king. She was so pleased that he had been born safely here in Mamlakat Almas.

He was crying very loudly and a nurse was wrapping him up and preparing to take him over to Adele.

'Can I take him?' Zahir asked her.

That would be a yes.

He took his baby and rested him in his arm. He looked down at his son, who stared back and calmed in such a firm hold.

Zahir went over to Adele and sat on the stool, putting the baby's head by hers and watching them meet.

And he saw tears flow freely from Adele's eyes.

He was the most beautiful baby, with navy eyes and thick black lashes and he didn't look like a newborn. He was stunning and he had her heart just like that.

And the name they had chosen was absolutely right, Adele thought as she felt his little fat hand reach out for his mother.

'Azzam...' Adele said, and she kissed him.

And later, much later, sitting in bed, holding her baby with Zahir by her side, the baby was introduced to his family and Leila finally got to know his name.

Azzam.

Royal Prince Sheikh Azzam Al Rahal, of Mamlakat Almas.

It would be stitched onto a little square tonight and placed in the centre of his blanket.

The palace healer also came to visit Adele and he thought she might need at least eight weeks of the healing baths.

'Maybe ten,' he said, and gave Adele a smile.

'Your mother will be delighted,' Adele said to her husband when the healer had left.

They were breaking one old tradition, though,

and Adele would be back in Zahir's bed on her first night home.

'Once you have finished your course in the healing baths, we shall have to see about a honeymoon.'

'Where?' Adele said.

'You choose.'

And she thought of an oasis in the desert but she would not be forgetting to take her Pill this time.

She could not have been happier.

Neither could Zahir.

And later, after she had fed him and Zahir was settling him down, she called Janet to share the happy news.

'It's a beautiful name,' Janet said. 'What does it mean?'

'It means determined,' Adele said, and then Zahir smiled at her and she met his gaze. He walked to Adele and sat on the bed, took her hand as she explained further.

'Resolved.'

* * * * *

Look out for the next great story in the
DESERT PRINCE DOCS *duet*

CHALLENGING THE DOCTOR SHEIKH
by Amalie Berlin

And if you enjoyed this story, check out
these other great reads from Carol Marinelli

SEDUCED BY THE HEART SURGEON
THE SOCIALITE'S SECRET
THE BABY OF THEIR DREAMS
JUST ONE NIGHT?

All available now!